"Jump, Lainie. I'll catch you," Rand promised, holding out his arms.

He was there, ten feet below her on the ground.

"How did you get there?" she demanded.

"There's a gate a few feet down the wall I decided to use."

"Rand Bennett! When I get my hands on you. . . !" She slid off the top of the wall and into his arms. Rand caught her easily, but deliberately let his knees buckle, and they both went tumbling onto the ground. Rand broke into gales of laughter. Unable to restrain a laugh herself, Lainie lightly punched Rand's arm. "I thought you said you'd catch me!"

"I did catch you," he protested. "But I didn't say I wouldn't fall doing it."

"Somehow, in some way, I will get you for this," she vowed ominously.

Rand's golden-brown eyes were shining into hers with such intensity, Lainie felt it was like looking directly into the sun. The effect was blinding.

"You can have me," he said softly, "anytime you want me . . ."

WHAT ARE *LOVESWEPT* ROMANCES?

They are stories of true romance and touching emotion. We believe those two very important ingredients are constants in our highly sensual and very believable stories in the *LOVESWEPT* line. Our goal is to give you, the reader, stories of consistently high quality that may sometimes make you laugh, sometimes make you cry, but are always fresh and creative and contain many delightful surprises within their pages.

Most romance fans read an enormous number of books. Those they truly love, they keep. Others may be traded with friends and soon forgotten. We hope that each *LOVESWEPT* romance will be a treasure—a "keeper." We will always try to publish

LOVE STORIES YOU'LL NEVER FORGET
BY AUTHORS YOU'LL ALWAYS REMEMBER

The Editors

LOVESWEPT® • 140

Fayrene Preston
Fire in the Rain

BANTAM BOOKS
TORONTO • NEW YORK • LONDON • SYDNEY • AUCKLAND

FIRE IN THE RAIN

A Bantam Book / May 1986

LOVESWEPT® and the wave device are registered trademarks of Bantam Books, Inc. Registered in U.S. Patent and Trademark Office and elsewhere.

ISBN 0-553-21758-5

Published simultaneously in the United States and Canada

Bantam Books are published by Bantam Books, Inc. Its trademark, consisting of the words "Bantam Books" and the portrayal of a rooster, is Registered in U.S. Patent and Trademark Office and in other countries. Marca Registrada. Bantam Books, Inc., 666 Fifth Avenue, New York, New York 10103.

PRINTED IN THE UNITED STATES OF AMERICA

O   0 9 8 7 6 5 4 3 2 1

This is dedicated to:
DANIEL
because he says novenas for me
And to his mother,
CAROL JERINA

One

With her shoulders hunched in what she thought could too easily become her permanent posture, Lainie Stewart automatically positioned two pieces of cotton polyester for the next seam. She had completed several hundred such seams today. And yesterday. And the day before. And she would do so again tomorrow.

The factory in Houston where she worked turned out less-than-exact replicas of women's sportswear from one of the country's leading lines. This past week Lainie had been working on skirts. A stack of precut pieces sat on her right, waiting for the straight seams required for each skirt. A stack on her left testified to the amount of work she had finished.

She used a heavy industrial sewing machine, tall spools of thread perched on its top. It operated at high speeds and could be dangerous to people who didn't know exactly what they were doing. But she did. She had worked for four years now in this small concrete building with its row after row of identical machines and its bare fluorescent tubes of light hanging from the ceiling. It was a noisy, dusty place. In the winter it was too cold, and in the summer it was too hot, but Lainie hardly noticed anymore. She was paid by the piece, and she concentrated on turning out as many as she could, hour after hour, day after day.

A lot of people might look down on what she did, but she was not ashamed. When her mother had died, she had eagerly taken her baby brother, Joey, to raise. With no training, not even a high school diploma, she had been grateful for the job, and she was grateful for it now. It was good, honest work, Lainie told herself, and, for the present anyway, it was the best conceivable means of support for Joey and herself.

She glanced at the clock. Another hour to go before she could quit. Her thoughts went to Joey as they so often did during the day. He was six years old now, and every day at this time the school bus deposited him in front of the pink stucco duplex where they lived. Rosa and her husband, Efrain, lived in the other half of the duplex; Rosa waited for Joey on the porch. After their ritual hug Joey skipped to their apartment, changed into his play clothes, then raced back to Rosa's kitchen for a glass of milk and a piece of fruit or a slice of cheese. It made Lainie feel better to know what he was doing at any given time, and if she couldn't be there for him, she was glad Rosa was.

Lainie had worked hard to structure a world of love and security for Joey, and that world certainly included Rosa. With her brown skin lined with age and her graying dark hair, the older woman was like a grandmother to him. Joey had confided that it was nice to be hugged by Rosa because she wasn't very tall, and she was padded all over. Plus, he had noted, she always smelled of the spices she used when she cooked. Joey thought hers was one of the best smells in the whole world.

Lainie knew just what he meant, for she had thought the very same thing about Rosa when she had been a little girl. Rosa had been her family's housekeeper and had given Lainie the same special welcome when she had come from school that she now gave Joey.

Lainie's lips curved into a tender smile just thinking about her little brother. He was very precious to her. He had given her life direction and meaning. Because of him, she had abandoned the wild crowd she had run around with for over two years, gone back to school at night, gotten her high school diploma, and was now taking college courses. She didn't plan to work forever in this garment factory.

In her mind she began ticking off the things she had to do when she got home. She had started a stew in the slow cooker this morning, so dinner would be taken care of. But she had washing to do, and then she planned to sew. At night in her dreams the tall stacks of pattern pieces waiting to be sewn never seemed to diminish. When she woke up and went to work, she found it was that way in real life too.

"Lainie."

Glancing around she saw Efrain hurrying toward her, wearing the same worried expression on his face that seemed to be there constantly. She smiled. The small wiry man was very dear to her. As the foreman of the garment factory he had helped her get a job here. And as a friend he saw to it that she got as much piecework to take home with her as she wanted.

"Efrain, can you get me a stack of pockets ready for tonight?" The pockets were to have a rose design appliquéd on them. It required more skill and time than the seams she did during the day, and thus paid more. She worked at it for a few hours every evening after Joey went to sleep, and she tried to complete several stacks a week.

"Lainie—"

"Also, I think you should check out this machine. The action on the knee press is getting sluggish."

"Lainie . . ."

The grave note in Efrain's voice finally reached her through the loud drone of the machines. "What's wrong?" she asked, and then came to her feet as cold fear struck into her heart. "Oh, my God, it's not Joey, is it?"

Efrain's dark eyes glistened with the beginning of tears. "Sí, querida. I am afraid it is. Rosa is on the phone. She's at the hospital. Joey, he's been hit by a car, and they don't know how serious it is. They want you to give verbal permission so they can begin treating him."

Lainie headed for Efrain's office at a dead run.

*   *   *

Dr. Rand Bennett had put in a grueling day that had started at five that morning when his alarm had gone off. He had arrived at the hospital by five-thirty, and from then on his day had consisted of one crisis after another. But now as he hung his white coat in his locker, he was through and, barring any unforeseen circumstances, he could look forward to a game of handball with one of the Emergency Room doctors, and later an evening out with a delightful young Houston socialite he knew he could count on to be good company both during and after dinner.

His schedule was hectic, but that was the way he preferred it. In fact, he thrived on it. Since his last trip to the Central American country of Montaraz over a year ago, he had concentrated his efforts to help people closer to home. Long ago he had learned that he couldn't change the world, but he could change little parts of it. Thus his clinic had been born, and it was just beginning to function really well. He tried to devote at least two afternoons a week to it.

Holding a cup of coffee in his hand, he sauntered through the Emergency Room looking for his colleague.

"Dr. Bennett."

Checking his stride, he threw a look over his shoulder toward the person calling his name, a pretty blond nurse who was manning the station. Her lips curved upward into an almost worshipful smile. Rand was used to that type of treatment and hardly noticed it. Sometimes it amused him, sometimes it annoyed him, but most of the time he didn't even think about it. There were just too many important things that required his attention. "Yes?"

"Dr. Kaufman said to tell you he'd meet you at the club. He had an opportunity to leave early."

"Thanks"—he glanced at her name tag—"Ms. Gray."

Taking another sip of coffee and absently telling himself he was consuming too much caffeine, he headed for the double doors of the ambulance entrance. They automatically opened before him. Rand took a step forward, then came to a complete stop. For in front of the emergency entrance a young woman was just getting out of a taxi. Simply dressed in a pair of faded jeans and a cream-colored T-shirt, she was, Rand thought, the most stunning woman he had ever seen. Slim and long-legged, she had coal-black hair, pulled back from her face and woven into a thick braid that hung nearly to her waist.

Unaware of him as yet, she rushed toward the entrance and rammed right into him, knocking the cup out of his hand and spilling the dark brown liquid down the front of his beige Polo shirt.

"Whoa!" he ordered, gripping her arms in a firm hold, and immediately deciding that whoever she was, she most certainly constituted an unforeseen circumstance. "You can't go running into the Emergency Room like that. Do you need help? Are you ill?"

Extraordinary jade eyes, fringed with the longest, darkest lashes he had ever seen, looked up beseechingly at him. "Please! I've got to find Joey! He's hurt!"

"Joey? You have a relative in the Emergency Room?"

Lainie didn't feel his hands on her arms. She only knew he was a tall, solid obstruction she had to get around. She struggled under his hands. "Yes! Joey, my brother! Get out of my way!"

"Calm down and I'll help you find him," Rand promised, surprising himself. Normally he would have directed anyone else to the nurse at the station. "What's your name?"

"Lainie Stewart, and my brother's name is Joey Gordon." She had only a vague impression of a long, lean body and golden-brown eyes. But it didn't matter to her in the slightest what the man standing in front of her looked like. If he could help her get to Joey, she would tell him anything he wanted to know. In the taxi coming to the hospital her imagination had painted terrible pictures in her head of what she would find when she arrived.

"Come on." Reluctant to relinquish his hold on her, he took her hand and guided her to the reception desk. "Ms. Gray, do you have a Joey Gordon here?"

The nurse remembered just in time to close her mouth, and Rand could almost read her mind. Unless it concerned one of his patients, no one dared bother Dr. Bennett, much less run into him and spill coffee down his shirt. In this instance her attitude annoyed him.

"This is his sister, Lainie Stewart," Rand prompted with an autocratic lift of one brow.

"Oh, yes." She immediately pulled herself together and gave Lainie an extremely professional smile. "I spoke with you on the phone when you gave us your consent." The nurse consulted her records. "He's in Trauma One. Dr. Daniels is checking his X rays now." She reached for a clipboard with forms on it and held it toward Lainie. "If you'll just fill these out, Dr. Daniels will see you as soon as he can."

Lainie gritted her teeth. Why couldn't these people understand? Joey was all she had in the world! "*No!* I want to see Joey now! Where's Trauma One?"

Rand squeezed Lainie's hand comfortingly. "Stay here and I'll go check on his condition. I promise I'll come back and give you a report in just a couple of minutes." He didn't understand why, but he knew that he would never willingly take this woman into a situation where it might make the anguish on her face worse than it was already.

"I'm coming with you," she insisted. "I need to see Joey. He's only a baby. Nothing can happen to him." There was no trace of hysteria in her voice, just a grim determination.

He hesitated, but the firm set of her jaw and the purposeful blaze in her eyes told him she would not be left behind. Still holding her hand, he began leading the way down the hall.

"But the forms . . ." Ms. Gray called after them.

"Later," he replied tersely. They went through the trauma unit door, but when they reached the curtained section that made up Trauma One, he stepped in front of her, using his body to block her vision. He peered through the gap in the curtain. Not until he assessed the condition within did he relax and move aside.

His control of the situation was barely noticeable, and Lainie didn't even think to object. She saw her little brother and rushed to his side. "Joey, oh, Joey!"

His blue eyes were large and frightened as he lay on the examining table, but they lighted up the instant he spotted Lainie, and he tried to get up.

"No, *niño*. Keep still now." Sitting beside the bed, Rosa exerted a firm staying pressure to his shoulder.

Lainie leaned down and laid a soft kiss on the bridge of his nose. It was a habit that had grown out of the first time she had ever held him. As a newborn his nose had been so tiny, she hadn't been able to resist; and ever since it had been her favorite place to kiss him. She knew all too well, though, that her days of being able to do it were numbered. When he got older, she would probably be lucky if he even tolerated a kiss on the cheek, "How are you, baby?"

"I don't feel good," he said, and hiccuped at the same time. Apparently he had cried so much that he was now reduced to hiccuping sobs.

"What happened?" she asked, gently combing her fingers through his fine, curly blond hair and thankfully finding no injury.

"A turtle." He hiccuped again. "Kyle found a turtle. I forgot I wasn't supposed to cross the street."

"A turtle?" While he was talking, Lainie inspected every inch of him. He looked so small and pathetic. His arms and legs, still chunky with baby fat, extended past the short hospital gown he wore. His skin had lost its usually rosy tone and had paled to the same shade of white as the gown.

The injuries she could see were all located on his left side—an ugly gash on his forehead and upper left arm and several bad scrapes down the side of his leg. His arm was held immobile by a board and had an ice pack on it. Her eyes flicked to Rosa with a question.

"I told him to go change into his play clothes as usual. While he was in your apartment, I heard his best friend, Kyle, shouting. I went to the window. Kyle was yelling to Joey for him to come see the turtle he had found. Before I could stop him, Joey ran out of the house and into the street. *Gracias a dios!* The car was not going fast. It hit him on his side and threw him against the curb."

"Lainie, I hurt."

Her heart clenched with pain at the sound of his little sobs. "I know, baby, but you're going to be all right." Without taking her eyes from him, she asked Rosa, "What has the doctor said?"

"He hasn't brought back the X rays, but he thinks Joey's left arm is broken."

"Lainie," he whimpered, and sounded as if he were going to begin crying again.

"Yes, honey, I'm here." She hovered over him, trying to think of a way to reassure him.

From behind her she heard a surprised and respectful voice. "Dr. Bennett! Can I help you?"

"I'm here with the boy's family. How are the X rays?"

"It's as I thought. There's a nondisplaced fracture of his left forearm."

Lainie had turned. "Is it bad?"

"This is Joey's sister," Rand explained. "Lainie Stewart."

Dr. Daniels nodded. "Joey was a lucky little boy. There doesn't appear to be any head or internal injuries. I'll need to suture those two lacerations, and we have an orthopedic man available, so we should be able to have his arm set in just a little while." His gaze encompassed both Lainie and Rosa. "If you would please wait in the reception area, someone will come for you when he's ready."

Joey started crying. Lainie desperately wanted to take him in her arms and hold him close, but if she did, she was afraid that it might cause him more pain. With all her heart she wished it were she lying there instead of him. "Don't cry, baby," she murmured. "Everything is going to be okay." To the doctor she said firmly, "I'm staying."

He was just as firm. "I'm sorry, but the patient must have one hundred percent of our attention. We can't be worried about how relatives will react. We lose more parents than we do children." He laughed at his own joke.

Lainie didn't laugh. "You won't have to worry about me. I'll be fine."

Rosa spoke up. "You let her stay, doctor. I'll leave. Lainie, I left the house in such a hurry, I think something is cooking on my stove. Now that I know Joey will be okay, I'll go home and get things ready for him."

Lainie walked around the bed to Rosa and gave her a hug. "Thank you. I don't know what I'd do without you. Just turn down his bed. He'll probably want to sleep when I get him home."

"I'm sure you're right." Rosa patted Lainie on the cheek. "Don't you worry, *querida.*" Then she bent down to kiss Joey. "Hush, now, don't cry," she whispered. "You be a good *niño*, and I'll see you when you get home."

Joey sniffed loudly. "Lainie, I want to go home too."

"In just a little bit, and in the meantime I won't leave you."

Dr. Daniels started to object again, but Rand cut in with quiet authority. "Let his sister stay. I'll be here with her, and if she faints, I'll catch her."

The younger doctor complied as Rand had known he would. Rand was used to getting his way. "Of course, Dr. Bennett."

Daniels obviously hadn't taken a good look at Lainie, Rand thought. For if he had, he would have seen for himself that she wasn't the type of woman to faint. Though she had flawless skin covering a delicate bone structure, there was a strength in her face that couldn't be denied. Coupled with her exotic coloring was a beauty that went beyond the ordinary. He moved to her and put his hand on her shoulder. To anyone looking it would appear that he was comforting her.

But Lainie felt the heat of his touch and stepped away. Up until now she had been only distantly aware of the man, who for some reason had been with her since she had entered the hospital. She had been so concerned about finding out how Joey was that the man had been another minor irritant, one more person to get through in order to reach Joey. But now she focused her attention on him.

He had a strong, intelligent face, with two deep lines that creased his cheeks vertically. His skin was tanned and had an almost weathered quality about it, as if in one period of his life he had spent a lot of time outdoors. His thick brown hair feathered across his forehead in such a way that she immediately decided he must have a hard time keeping it neatly combed. And knowing what she did of him—by reputation only, of course—she decided he probably didn't care whether his hair was neatly combed or not.

For that was the man's way, Lainie told herself. He was a law unto himself, a man who made paths where others had never dared travel. He was Dr. Rand Bennett, and it was a measure of how upset she had been that she hadn't recognized him before now. He appeared regularly in the newspapers and on television, conducting news conferences concerning a famous patient or a new technique in heart surgery, or both. What was he doing here? she wondered. Her eyes lowered to his coffee-stained shirt. She seemed to remember running into him. Her forehead wrinkled briefly, then smoothed. She couldn't worry about it now.

Dr. Daniels was speaking to her brother. "Joey, I'm going to give you something that will make you feel a whole lot better. Then we'll fix you up, and you'll be home in your own bed before you know it. Doesn't that sound good?" At that moment a nurse walked in carrying a small tray.

Joey was not fooled. "Is that a shot?" His voice was wavering toward panic.

Lainie experienced a familiar helplessness. With every trip to the doctor she and Joey went through the same routine—him becoming nearly hysterical at just the thought of a needle and her trying to comfort him. Lainie's knowing that this particular injection would calm him down and ease his pain didn't make it any easier for her to bear his fears.

Rand nudged Lainie away from her brother's bedside and motioned the nurse to begin. He took Joey's hand. "Hi, my name's Rand, and I'm a doctor in this hospital. I'd like to be your friend."

"Is that a shot?" Joey was single-minded.

"Yes, it is," he answered without hesitation. It wasn't his way to lie, especially to a child. "You're going to feel just a little sting, but I'll be right here with you." Fresh tears welled up in Joey's eyes, and the nurse began swabbing a sterile area on his upper thigh. "Just keep holding my hand and count with me, okay? Ten. Joey, say ten." The number ten came out of the little boy's mouth on a ragged sob. "Good! Now, nine." Joey repeated nine. "Eight," Rand said and squeezed his hand tightly as the little boy let out a scream. "Hey, it's all over! How about that?" Rand gently rubbed the spot where the needle had gone in. "And now you're going to feel all better."

He had the most soothing voice, Lainie thought. It could catch a person unawares, just as it had Joey. And while she couldn't help but be a little indignant that he had usurped her place with her brother, she was nevertheless grateful.

Joey had stopped crying and was looking with interest at the man who had played that number game with him while he had gotten the awful shot. "You're a doctor?" Rand nodded. "Doctors take care of people, don't they?"

Rand laughed softly. "They sure do, Joey."

"Lainie?" Joey called, and she came into his view

at once. When Rand began moving away from the bed, he said, "Don't go."

"I won't," Rand assured, and with a light touch to her shoulder, moved her into the position he had had. "I'll stay right here with your sister."

Joey looked at Lainie and then at the man who had helped him, who had held his hand so that the shot wouldn't hurt so bad. The two of them were standing side by side, just like they were friends. They looked real nice together, Joey decided drowsily. "Good," he murmured, and closed his eyes as the medication began to take effect. "Stay. Both of you."

Two

Lainie felt almost as battered as Joey looked by the time Dr. Daniels and the orthopedic doctor got through working on him. Joey was doing fine, however. The medication had relaxed him and taken away the pain, and the plaster on his cast had almost dried.

A nurse handed her a set of written instructions. "If you'd like to go get your car, we'll bring Joey out to you in a wheelchair."

"Oh!" Lainie's hand went to her forehead in consternation. She'd forgotten about the problem of getting them home. She had no car. Rosa and Efrain had a car, but Rosa had kept it today, and as it turned out, it had been a good thing, because she had used it to bring Joey to the hospital and to drive herself back home. "I came in a cab."

"Would you like me to call you another one?" the nurse asked.

"Uh . . ." Lainie tried to think. The unexpected cab fare had taken all of the cash she had had in her purse. She would just have to call Rosa to come back to the hospital and get them.

"There's no need to bother with a taxi," Rand interjected smoothly. "I'll take you home." To the nurse he said, "Get hold of my assistant and tell her to cancel both my afternoon and my evening engagements." As the nurse hurried away, he turned to the resident who had assisted Dr. Daniels. "I'll have my car in front of the entrance in two minutes."

"Excuse me." Lainie's voice was cool but polite. "There's no need to go to any trouble. I'll just call—"

A smile softened the firm lines of his mouth. "It's no trouble."

His stance was remarkably casual, Lainie noticed with amazement, but that was deceptive, because the air surrounding him absolutely crackled with energy, and that energy touched all those around him, galvanizing them to do his bidding. A man who could electrify the very molecules in the air while simply standing still, was a man definitely to be avoided, she reasoned.

"No, really—"

"Two minutes," he repeated to the resident, then strode off.

Lainie watched him go, astounded by the way he seemed to sweep people before him. "Is Dr. Bennett always that highhanded?"

Dr. Daniels grinned. "With almost everyone

except his patients. But then again, with the miracles he performs, he's entitled to be highhanded."

Not with me, he isn't! Lainie thought, greatly irritated. Yet in the next instant, she shrugged it off. She had a personal rule against worrying about things that weren't of vital importance to either her or Joey. In the overall scheme of things accepting a ride from Dr. Rand Bennett didn't fall into either category. The car ride would last only fifteen minutes, twenty at the most, and it would allow her to get Joey home faster than if they had to wait for Rosa. With the matter settled in her mind, she turned her attention back to Joey.

By the time they arrived home, Joey had fallen asleep in Lainie's arms. Used to managing for herself, she reached for the car door handle, intending to carry Joey.

"Stay where you are," Rand instructed. "I'll come around and get him for you."

She didn't argue. She felt greatly conflicted about the presumptuous Dr. Bennett. She was grateful to the point of tears that he had intervened so she could stay with Joey in the Emergency Room. Yet he was so bossy that he set her teeth on edge. Oh, well. What did it matter? she reasoned. In just a few minutes Dr. Rand Bennett would be gone from her life anyway.

Once inside the apartment she decided that as long as he was here, she might as well take full advantage of him. She pointed toward the bedroom. "If you don't mind, will you carry him in there for me?"

"I had intended to," he answered with the assuredness that was beginning to annoy Lainie more and more. However, she controlled it, reminding herself that getting her brother settled was the most important thing. Once in Joey's room, they discovered that Rosa had turned back the covers as requested, and Rand gently settled the little boy into the bed. "Do you have some extra pillows?" he asked quietly. "We need to elevate his arm."

She nodded. Opening the closet door, she pulled out the two pillows she used every night when she slept on the living room sofa and handed them to him. Tonight she could do without pillows, she told herself.

Without disturbing him, Rand moved around the bed, carefully placing Joey and his arm in the most comfortable position possible. Lainie watched with mixed feelings. While it was very reassuring to have a doctor see to it that Joey was settled just right, it was odd to have a man in her home. Particularly this man. She had arranged the apartment for her and Joey, with no room for a man. But strangely, Rand Bennett did fit, and she couldn't understand why, unless he was just the type of man who was at home wherever he went.

In the car driving home from the hospital, Lainie had begun recalling bits and pieces of information she had heard about him at various times. She could remember his name being associated with a clinic for the underprivileged in Houston, a jungle in Central America, and a family estate on Philadelphia's Main Line. There was no doubt about it. He was an interesting man—even an attractive man—but he was also a man she wanted no part of.

As Rand straightened he caught sight of the most disreputable-looking teddy bear he had ever seen, lying at the foot of the bed. One of its eyes was missing, and all of its appendages appeared to have been sewn on more than once, if the different colors of thread that appeared at every seam was anything to go by. But there was something about the silly bear that appealed to him, and he picked it up, casting a questioning glance at Lainie.

"That's Bunny Bear," she said softly. "When Joey was about eighteen months old, I took him shopping, intending to buy him a stuffed animal for Easter. I showed him all kinds of stuffed rabbits, but he didn't respond to any of them. Then he saw this bear, and he nearly jumped out of my arms, he was so eager to get his little hands on it. From that day on they've been inseparable."

She took the bear from Rand and tucked it under Joey's good arm. Without waking, the little boy turned his cheek into the fuzzy head of his bear. Watching him, Lainie blinked away tears that momentarily threatened. After the scare of his accident she couldn't begin to describe how thankful she was to have Joey back in his own bed. Dropping a tender kiss on his cheek, she whispered, "Sleep well, my baby."

Back in the living room, Lainie's temporarily gentle mood disappeared as Rand said, "He should sleep fine now, though just as a precaution you'll need to wake him every couple of hours throughout the night and talk with him. Tomorrow he'll probably feel a little achy. You're allowed to give him an aspirin substitute."

"Yes, that's what the instruction sheet said . . . the one that I was given at the hospital."

Rand raised his eyebrows at Lainie's restrained tone, for the first time realizing he had a problem. She didn't like being told what to do, and unfortunately giving orders was second nature to him. He was going to have to tread very carefully. He wasn't sure why, but it was important to him that he not make a bad impression with her. Telling himself he would figure out the reasons later, he said simply, "I'm sorry. I know better than anyone that I can be terribly overbearing. My only excuse is that sometimes it's hard to turn off being a doctor."

His confession was disarming, as she was sure he had intended it to be. Nevertheless, she didn't plan to give an inch. She fixed her cool jade eyes on him. "I'm sorry too. You've been very kind, and I can't thank you enough. But if you don't mind, I'm rather tired."

"Yes, I can see that." On impulse he reached out to brush away a strand of glistening black hair that had come loose from her braid and fallen forward across her cheek, but she jerked her head away before he could touch her.

He frowned. Whether it was patients he was treating or women he was seeing, *no one* ever jerked away from his touch. Lainie Stewart certainly presented a challenge. She wanted him to leave, he knew that. But, dammit, if he left now before he could break through that hard core of remoteness she was using as a shield against him, he might never have another chance. A moment's curiosity made him wonder if she reacted that way to all men, but a surprising spear of jealousy made him discard the idea of Lainie and any other man.

Stalling for time, he looked around the room and decided that he liked what he saw. The apartment might be small and cheaply furnished, but it was bright, cheerful, and homey. And clean, despite the various toys scattered around. It was a place where a little boy could be happy. Rand approved—and wished he didn't. He supposed it was because Lainie Stewart appeared to be so self-sufficient, so self-contained. He would feel a lot better if she seemed to need something, someone—*him*. It was an odd reaction, he admitted, particularly considering they had had such a short acquaintance. It was also a reaction he had never had before.

A grouping of photographs on a side table caught Rand's attention, and he walked over to look at them. As he had expected, there were several of Joey at various ages. And there was one of the woman who had been sitting beside Joey in the trauma unit when they had arrived. A man was standing beside her with his arm around her, and they were smiling contentedly into the camera.

Then he found one of Lainie and Joey. Picking it up, he ran a finger over the two laughing people in the picture. They were both sitting in a field of bluebonnets, Joey in front of his sister, she with her arms around him. Her hair was loose, blowing free in the wind, and there were wildflowers stuck behind her left ear. He would love to see her like that, he thought. Happy and unguarded.

Lainie watched the way he touched the picture. His fingers were slender and long; his hands showed strength and cleverness. She could easily see how his hands could be capable of great things. With a scalpel they could cut; with sutures they could close a wound; with their knowledge they could heal. And no doubt, with a single stroke on a woman's skin, they could raise desire. Rand Bennett was a brilliant and skilled man, she reminded herself, and she wanted him out of her home.

Even with his back to her, Rand could feel Lainie's desire to have him gone. There was nothing left for him to do. He would leave, he decided. A sigh of regret escaped his lips as he picked up the last of the photographs. It was of a different woman. Standing all alone under a tree, she had a faraway look in her eyes and a faded, delicate beauty. She and Lainie didn't resemble each other in the slightest, but he knew without asking it must be her mother. "She's lovely," he murmured, "and she looks very gentle, as if a butterfly might light in her hand and not be frightened." He replaced the picture on the table, and turned, ready to say, "I'll go."

But then it happened. Lainie *smiled* at him, truly smiled, and all thoughts of leaving her fled from his mind. He was convinced that just the memory of a smile like that would make a dark day brighter.

"Thank you," she said, moved by his remark about her mother. "That's my mother, Alice. She died when Joey was two. I miss her very much." Having said far more than she had intended in those few sentences, she cast about for another subject, then once more noticed his stained shirt.

"I should apologize for spilling coffee on you. I wasn't looking where I was going. If the stain won't come out, let me know and I'll replace the shirt."

"Forget it," he said softly, knowing that she would probably be hard pressed to fit the purchase of a Polo shirt into her budget, but impressed that she offered. "It's not important." *What now?* he wondered. *What can I do so that she won't ask me to leave?* From where he was standing he could see the kitchen and a small eating area. The two areas were divided by a bar. A hearty aroma drifted out to him. "What smells so good?"

"Oh, it's just a stew." She dismissed it with a little laugh and glanced toward Joey's bedroom door. "It was supposed to be for dinner."

His expressive brows drew together. "What do you mean, supposed to be? You still need to eat—and if I remember correctly, I don't think I had any lunch."

Lainie walked into the kitchen, mainly to give herself time to think. *What should I do?* He obviously had no intention of leaving, at least not easily. And for all intents and purposes he had just invited himself to dinner.

She grabbed a wooden spoon and lifted the lid of the cooker. Rand Bennett was definitely the most arrogant man she had ever met, but two things were stopping her from throwing him out. One—as Dr. Daniels had said, maybe he was entitled, just for tonight at any rate. After all, he had given her an awful lot of help with Joey. And two—Rosa would never understand if she turned away someone who was hungry from her home. Rosa had drilled manners and hospitality into her. If there was only one bean left in the pot, you shared it.

She turned to find that he had followed her. His lean muscular body filled the doorway of the kitchen, and although several feet away from her, she could feel the power of his magnetism from where she stood. She gave in and gestured toward the pot of stew. "It's not much, but you're welcome to stay and have some if you like."

"I accept." His twinkling eyes and wry grin told her that he had seen the struggle she had had over the decision of whether or not to ask him to stay. "If you'll let me set the table," he added.

"You must have been raised by someone like Rosa," Lainie said, smiling in spite of herself. The famous Dr. Bennett setting her tiny kitchen table with her cracked pottery appealed to her sense of the ridiculous.

Unerringly he went to the cabinet that held the dishes and pulled out two. "Rosa? Oh, I remember. The lady who was with Joey when we arrived."

He put the plates on the table, then came back and pointed inquiringly to a drawer that held the knives, forks, and spoons. Nodding grudgingly, she watched as he pulled out two sets of each. Totally at ease in her little apartment, he appeared unable to make a single awkward movement.

"If you're talking about someone teaching me to set the table when I'm invited to dinner, then no." He paused. "Uh, what do we have to drink?"

He certainly was being free with his *we*'s, Lainie thought, losing some of her amusement. "Tea. In the refrigerator." She didn't even offer to show him where the glasses were. Somehow she knew he would find them, and he did.

"You see," he went on, evidently enjoying himself, "I had what is commonly known as a privileged upbringing."

"How privileged?"

"Old money, lots of it. Old family retainers, lots of them. Old houses . . . well, not lots, but—"

"Don't tell me, let me guess." Her tone was dry, accepting. "Old houses—big."

He flashed her a look filled with humor, before deftly pouring tea into two tall glasses. "Enormous. I was raised to have excruciatingly proper manners. Fortunately or unfortunately, depending on how you look at it, I manage successfully to forget most of them for great periods of time. As for my learning to set a table, I suppose that's one of those skills one somehow acquires here or there."

Here or there. Lainie's mind picked up images of him setting the table for countless intimate dinners for two with scores of beautiful women. Shaking her head, she forced the images away and reached for two bowls. Ladling them full of the stew, it dawned on her all at once that she was starving. The stew, made with ground meat, was Joey's favorite. Glancing at the amount left in the pot, she judged there would be plenty for tonight, plus enough left over for Joey's lunch tomorrow.

She carried the bowls to the table and placed them on the center of each plate, then stood back to look critically at the table. Rand had already found the paper napkins. Naturally. "The bread! That's what's missing. I'm afraid all I have is sliced bread. Will that be okay?"

"Perfect." He waited while she got the loaf and brought it back to the table, then pulled out the chair for her.

With Rand Bennett sitting across the table from her, Lainie found that she couldn't say if the stew was good or not. Despite her determination to the contrary, the man definitely affected her. The disturbing energy she had noticed at the hospital seemed to be with him all the time. Watching him covertly, she decided it wasn't anything he consciously did. It was just there, a part of the man, as was his unrelenting male charm and sensuality. All the more reason to be wary of him, she reminded herself.

After a few minutes of eating, Rand commented curiously, "You and Joey have completely different coloring. You must each resemble your respective fathers."

"Not really." She hated even to think of Spence Gordon, Joey's father. A shiver ran through her, and to control it she reminded herself that Spence was completely out of their lives. Still, it was an effort to keep her voice steady. "Although I do carry my father's coloring, Joey has my mother's."

"You said your mother had died?" Without looking up from her plate, Lainie nodded. "And your stepfather also?" he asked.

"He's alive," she murmured tonelessly, finding a bite-size potato and pushing it around in the bowl. Her braid slipped forward over her shoulder, and she flung it back.

"Does he give you any help? Raising a child, a young boy, on your own is quite a responsibility."

She lifted her eyes to him. "I love Joey." She was

aware that she hadn't really answered his question, but it was all she planned to say on the matter. Glancing at his bowl, she saw it was nearly empty. It was her chance to change the subject and she took it. "Have some more stew."

"Thanks, I will." He helped himself to a second bowl of stew, all the while watching her. *Elegant, remote, desirable,* were words that described Lainie Stewart to perfection. She wore cotton and denim. He would love to dress her in silk. Jade silk. And then he would love to undress her.

But not yet, he thought. It was far too soon. "How old were you when your mother died?"

Lainie almost ground her teeth together. Perhaps it was Joey's accident. Perhaps it was because Spence's name had been brought into the conversation. Or perhaps it was something about Rand Bennett himself. But whatever the reason, she felt on edge, as if someone had methodically exposed all the nerves in her body and was slowly running a knife blade across the tips. She wasn't used to answering questions about her personal life, and she didn't like it. Yet because of the strangely compelling effect Rand seemed to have on her, she answered, "Twenty-one."

"It must have been hard on you."

She didn't want his or anyone's sympathy. "If you're referring to my taking Joey to raise, there was no hardship involved. I wanted him very badly, and I had been on my own for four years."

"You mean, in college?"

She smiled, a bitter smile. He just wouldn't let it drop. "I mean, running wild. When my mother remarried, I dropped out of school, left home, and took up serious partying as an occupation. I was very good at it."

She's trying to shock me, he thought, by telling me of her youthful rebellion. What she didn't realize was that he was totally shockproof. He had done and seen things that would curl that long beautiful hair of hers. These last years, his pioneering techniques in heart surgery had tended to overshadow the less savory parts of his past. He never forgot, however, and every once in a while it was brought back again. If it hadn't been for Alex Doral. . . . He looked at Lainie. Did she know? he wondered. And if not, would it make any difference to her if she found out?

He swallowed another spoonful of stew. "This is wonderful, Lainie. I can't remember when I've enjoyed a meal more."

His words were perfectly ordinary, yet a scream had begun to build inside her. She felt threatened but didn't know why. Long ago she had cut all men out of her life. Rand Bennett would be no exception. Tilting her head to one side, she regarded Rand with a resentful gaze. He probably used that same wonderful, deep voice on his patients to calm them out of their fears. But, she told herself emphatically, she wasn't afraid of him, and she refused to be charmed by him.

"Do you have a cook?" she asked with as much control as she could manage.

"Yes."

"And you probably eat in four- and five-star restaurants quite often?"

He lifted one eyebrow, wondering what she was getting at. "Sometimes."

"Then either you're lying, or you have very unusual taste buds."

He laid down his spoon and pushed away his plate. "Which do you think it is?" he asked quietly.

His eyes had narrowed on her, and her breath caught in her throat. The golden brown color of them was a lethal combination—rich, brilliant, and intense. "I'd like to think you're lying."

"Why?"

Rand's *why* had been softly spoken, but to her it sounded as loud as the low boom of thunder that at that moment was rumbling over the house. It was the first time she had been aware of the storm. Jumping up, she went to the window and looked out. Lightning scored the black sky and rain began to beat against the window. A spring storm. They were sometimes fast and unexpected, Lainie mused. Like life. Like Rand Bennett.

"Why, Lainie?" He had come to stand behind her. "Why would you like to think that I'm lying?"

The answer to his question was *Because I don't want to like you too much.* But because she couldn't tell him that, she wrapped her arms around her body and said, "The meal I served you was very simple fare. I don't need false compliments."

Her voice was so low that he barely heard her over the storm. Closing his hands over her shoulders, he turned her to face him. "What?"

She could feel the individual pressure of each of his fingers through the material of her T-shirt, and her heart began to hammer. "I don't have time for a lot of garbage in my life, Rand."

His brow pleated into a frown. "And you think I do?"

"I don't know. That's just it!" Her jade eyes flashed her frustration. "Rand, I heard you giving orders to cancel two engagements so that you could bring Joey and me home."

"So?"

He seemed so damn calm, she thought, but was he really? Hadn't the pressure of his fingers just increased? Certainly it felt as though the storm outside had taken up residence inside her body. *"What are you doing here?"*

He waited until another roll of thunder passed overhead. His thumbs slid along her collarbone and up either side of her neck. "Would you believe me if I told you that I'm not entirely sure? But from the moment I saw you stepping out of the cab at the hospital, getting to know you has been a compulsion with me."

"Lesser mortals are driven by compulsions," she scoffed, beginning to tremble under his touch. "Not the great Dr. Rand Bennett."

"Somehow I didn't think you'd believe me. So why don't I show you?" With movements that were easy, smooth, and hypnotizing, he took her braid and very slowly wrapped its length around his hand until his palm was right up against the back of her head. Then he lowered his mouth to hers.

Hard. That was how he was kissing her, she realized dimly. As if he had been wanting to kiss her since he had first seen her. And *seductively.* As if he wanted her to stop resisting him, open her mouth, and allow him more. It worked.

His tongue dipped into her mouth, joining hers, and any objectivity she had been trying to hold on to slipped right away. There was hunger in his kiss, and her body reverberated with the shock of it—shock, because she found she desperately wanted to feed that hunger. His free hand went to her waist, pulling her tightly against him. She had never been kissed like this before. It was like the wildest roller-coaster ride she had ever taken. It was like the hottest fire she had ever felt.

He worked her T-shirt free, so that he could slide his hand beneath it and knead the soft flesh of her back. She moaned. It seemed unreal, this desire, this need. It had come up so fast. Like the storm outside.

His lips tore away from her mouth and skimmed over her heated cheek to her ear. "I don't want to leave, Lainie," he muttered huskily. "Don't ask me to leave." His tongue darted into her ear, and his hand traveled around to close over her breast.

She took a deep breath, tried to answer, but found herself unable to. She clung to him, her fingers digging into the hard muscles of his shoulders. Her lips parted, seeking, and she turned her head until he took possession of her lips once again. Incredibly there was no thought involved. Nothing but devastating feeling and hot, searing passion that went on and on, coiling deeper and deeper into her.

And it was affecting him the same way. She could feel his response. Yet it was he who drew away, pulling deep ragged gulps of air into his lungs. Slowly, reluctantly, he unwound her hair from around his hand. "I knew it would be like that. I don't know how, but I did."

She shook her head, totally undone by her reaction to him. "I'm not looking for a lover, Rand."

"No," he agreed, "but it doesn't seem to matter, does it? I wasn't looking for you either, yet somehow we've found each other."

She began edging away from him. "It's not going to happen, Rand."

"Maybe not tonight," he agreed, mentally cursing the guarded, wary look now in her eyes. Never quite open to him anyway—except maybe for those brief heated moments in his arms—she had closed up before him like some exotic flower folding in on itself to protect its heart.

With her hip Lainie hit one of the kitchen chairs and she was forced to stop. Angry with herself that she had showed him any weakness, she raised her chin. "Please go."

He shook his head. "Not yet, Lainie. We need to talk about what's happening between us."

The tip of her tongue flicked over her lips, and she regretted it instantly. The taste of him was still there. "You're right. Something *did* happen. But it's past, and talking about it will serve no purpose."

Casually, with the intent of seeming less threatening to her, he stuck his hands in his pockets, but at the same time, he took a step nearer to her. "Avoiding it, Lainie? Somehow I think that's not like you."

She had noticed both of his actions. "It's not. But with regard to this particular subject, discussing it will serve no purpose. You see, whatever was happening between us has stopped."

"Really? I hadn't noticed."

He was being arrogant right to the end, and she

had had enough. "Rand, this is my home, and I'm asking you to leave."

With his eyes on his shoes he pondered the situation. To a certain extent he knew he had led a charmed life. In school, athletics and studies had come easily; in his profession he had had an abundance of success, fame, and satisfaction; in his personal life he had been blessed with good friends and willing women. But now, tonight, he found himself in the position of having to face the fact that the one person, the one relationship, that might turn out to be the most important of his life, was not going to come to him easily.

Looking up, Rand became entangled in the jade depths of her eyes. To win her would take time, patience, and skill. He could handle it, he decided. He had a feeling that making Lainie Stewart his just might be the single most rewarding thing he had ever done in his life.

"I hate leaving you alone," he said softly.

"I'm used to being alone."

"That's a shame." His desire to pull her back to him was so strong, he could actually feel a strain in the muscles of his arms. He straightened. "I'll leave. But before I go, let's wake up Joey and check on him."

Joey. Lainie instantly switched gears. In spite of her desire to have Rand gone, she couldn't help but be glad that he was going to be with her the first time she woke her brother. She didn't care what the doctor had said at the hospital. Joey had that bad gash on his forehead and a concussion was obviously a possibility.

She clicked on the small light by the bed and knelt down. Rand did the same on the other side.

"Joey, honey, wake up." She shook his shoulder lightly. "Joey."

Slowly he opened his eyes and blinked at her. It was hard to keep the relief out of her voice. "Hi, sweetie. How are you?"

"Yuck-y."

"The shot's still in effect," Rand murmured.

Joey rolled his head toward the sound of Rand's voice and incredibly managed a little smile.

Rand's mouth relaxed into an answering grin. Children had always been a weakness with him, but he found himself being drawn to this little boy in particular. "Hi, buddy."

"You're still here." Joey's words were jumbled.

"I sure am. Can you remember what happened to you?"

Momentary confusion clouded the little boy's face, then cleared. "The turtle."

Rand glanced at Lainie. "That must have been some turtle. I would have liked to have seen it myself."

"A car," Joey said, his eyes closing.

She laid her hand on Joey's head. "You can go back to sleep now, honey. I'll be right in the next room if you need me. Okay?"

Joey didn't answer. He was already asleep, his Bunny Bear cradled in his good arm.

In the next room Rand caught the worried expression on her face. "He's going to be fine, Lainie. Kids bounce back fast."

She sighed. "I know. But when he hurts, I hurt."

And strangely enough, he thought, *When you*

hurt, I hurt. He wanted to tell her that he would stay the night so that he could be with her when she woke Joey up every two hours. But he knew she would refuse his offer. So he delved into his pocket, pulled out a pen and a card, wrote a number on the back of it, and handed it to her. "If for any reason you think Joey is having problems, call me. *Any* reason, Lainie, no matter how trivial you think it might be. If you get worried, call me. If you just want to talk, call me."

Even knowing that she would never use the phone number, she took the card and stared, fascinated by the boldly scrawled numbers. Feeling his fingers under her chin, she lifted her head and then she wished she hadn't, because she would rather not have seen the gentle, caring look in his eyes.

"Good night," he said, and placed a soft, sweet kiss on her lips.

"Good night."

He opened the door and walked out into the now subdued spring rain.

Touching her lips, Lainie told herself that the only reason she felt a sudden urge to cry was because she had been through a traumatic experience that had involved Joey, and quite naturally her defenses were down. But the fact remained, Rand had given her an incredibly tender kiss.

She wasn't used to tenderness from a man, and she wasn't used to a man's touch. Yet Rand Bennett had been touching her all night long. Tenderly.

Three

The night seemed long and lonely and silent. Sleep proved impossible for Lainie. Her mind was too busy.

As she watched Joey sleep her thoughts returned again and again to Rand. It had been odd the way that Joey had taken to him. Not that Joey wasn't normally a friendly child, yet his reaction to Rand had seemed a bit out of the ordinary. But then, she remembered irritably, she herself had all but dissolved at his kiss. In just a few hours Rand had had an enormous impact on both their lives. But surely, she tried to assure herself, it was only because he had caught them at their most vulnerable. It didn't mean a thing.

Still, Rand Bennett was obviously a very charismatic man, who, if he chose to exert his charms, could beguile even the most resistant of people. He was also a man who could threaten a woman's independence. And independence was something Lainie prized greatly.

It hadn't always been that way. As an only child she had been doted on by two parents who had loved her and each other very much. Her childhood had been idyllic, filled with laughter and security. But when she was fifteen, all the laughter stopped. Her father died, and without him, her mother was lost. He had been Alice's strength, and she had depended on him for everything. Just how much was brought home to Lainie two weeks after her father's funeral. She could still vividly recall how she had found her mother sitting at the kitchen table staring in bewilderment at the stack of monthly bills in front of her; suddenly she had realized her mother had no idea even how to go about paying bills.

Over the next couple of years Lainie tried in every way she knew to help, but it was frustrating, because she quickly learned that her mother needed more than she could provide.

Lainie grew into a high-spirited, volatile young beauty. Unfortunately her mother was incapable of providing any guidance. At a time in her life when she needed love and direction the most, Lainie got little. For when she was seventeen, her mother met Spence Gordon, a younger, good-looking man who was a pilot for a local commuter airline. Alice was completely bowled over by him. Lainie disliked him on sight.

At that age Lainie hadn't been able to voice exactly why she distrusted him so. He certainly didn't do anything obvious where she could say to her mother, "There. See that!" It was just that to Lainie he seemed too smooth, too eager to please.

Unable to see her mother marry a man she knew would hurt her, Lainie reacted in her own way. Rebelling with a vengeance, she left both home and school. Like a firecracker exploding, she flew off in all directions and got caught up with a fast crowd, whose main interest in life was serious partying. She burned the candle at both ends, working as a waitress, but earning only enough so that she could pay the rent on the small apartment she shared with four other girls.

She tried to stay close to her mother, to visit her often, but it wasn't always possible to guess when Spence would be gone, and more times than not, he was there. Lainie began to suspect that he took great pains to plan it that way. She had a feeling that he was afraid she would take the opportunity of being alone with Alice to turn her against him. What he probably didn't know was that she had tried many times and failed. With every day that passed, Alice became more and more dependent on Spence.

Her father had left her mother enough money and property so that she should have been comfortable for the rest of her life. But as soon after their marriage as possible, Alice turned over all her financial affairs to Spence, and within the next couple of years he managed to go through the entire legacy. During this time he lost his job and showed no inclination to get another one. His behavior became more and more erratic. Eventually Alice even had to let Rosa go. Then she got pregnant.

With the loss of the money and the advent of the baby, things began to change. Spence was suddenly gone for longer and longer periods of time—absences he never bothered to explain. For the first time in a long while her mother needed her and began to lean more and more on her. Lainie tried to be there for her. Yet no matter how she tried, she couldn't shake the feeling that she was failing her mother, because no matter what she did, it wasn't enough.

Even the birth of Joey didn't help. Her mother just seemed to fade away. And Lainie had to face the fact that her mother was a woman who flourished only under a man's care. Once that care was removed, Alice was too gentle to survive the realities of life alone. She grew weaker and weaker.

Lainie supposed it was then that her fiercely independent streak was born. Two years later, at the age of twenty-one and on the day of her mother's funeral, Lainie scooped Joey into her arms and walked out the door. Spence hadn't said a word. Not then, at any rate.

Coffee cup in hand, Lainie wandered to the window and gazed out. If the early morning was anything to go by, the day would be clear and bright. She took a sip of coffee and felt the warm liquid against her lips. Was it her imagination, she wondered, or were her lips still tingling from Rand's kiss? She put a hand to her mouth. Last night he had more or less forced himself into their lives, and during the short time he had been with them, he had taken her through a series of emotions that both baffled and frightened her. Rand was the first man to kiss her in over four years, and she couldn't seem to stop thinking about him.

A knock on the door jolted her out of her disturbing thoughts. It was Rosa. One look at the dark circles under Lainie's eyes and she threw her hands in the air, exclaiming, "*Por dios*. My poor little girl! You look terrible. Did Joey have a bad night?"

"Joey had a great night," Lainie answered wryly. "He would have slept straight through if it hadn't been for me waking him up every two hours."

Rosa bustled into the kitchen. It was a room where, no matter whose house it was, she felt truly at home. Automatically she reached for the skillet. "You sit back and rest. I'll make Joey some of those special eggs that he likes so much." She cast a sharp glance over her shoulder as Lainie slumped down at the kitchen table. "And you'll eat some too."

"No, really, I couldn't eat a thing."

"You'll eat," Rosa stated firmly in the voice she had used on her since Lainie was a toddler, "and then you'll go next door and sleep. Efrain said you are not to go in to work today. You sleep. I'll stay here and watch Joey."

She was not about to argue, Lainie decided. A short nap would be heaven.

Rosa leaned into the refrigerator and came up with a handful of ingredients. "I heard a car drive up last night." Her tone was casual. "I looked out the window and saw the doctor from the hospital bringing you and Joey home. You know," she prompted as if Lainie might not remember who had brought her home. "The *hermoso* one!"

"The handsome one!" Lainie smiled, then sat patiently, waiting for what she knew would come.

"At the hospital I took one look and said to myself, *'Muy macho!'* Don't you agree?" Rosa asked hopefully, but when Lainie remained silent, she went on determinedly. "So how long did he stay anyway?"

She knows to the minute, Lainie thought with a weary amusement. "Not long."

"I hope you fed him. Your cooking is good. I know! I taught you myself! I say to Efrain, 'Some man will be lucky to get her.' "

Watching Rosa's energetic preparations, Lainie hoped Joey's stomach was up to Rosa's eggs. With her mind obviously on another matter, namely Rand Bennett, Rosa was putting everything into the omelet she could find—green peppers, onions, celery, bologna. Lainie only just managed to save last night's leftover stew by snatching it away. "That's for Joey's lunch."

Rosa abandoned the omelet, planted her hands on her generous hips, and glared at Lainie. "I say to Efrain, 'It's been too long. She doesn't even date!' "

She needs a man, Lainie said to herself.

"I say to him, 'She needs a man,' " Rosa huffed.

And Efrain agreed, Lainie silently recited.

"And Efrain agreed," Rosa stated emphatically.

Lainie knew by heart Rosa's opinions on her single status. She also knew Rosa wasn't even half-way through her speech.

She didn't have to fake the yawn. "You know, I don't think I can stay awake a minute more. If you were really serious, I think I'll take you up on your offer and go over to your place to try to sleep."

Rosa wrung her hands, her expression reflecting both distress over Lainie's lack of sleep and disappointment that she wouldn't get to finish her lecture. Distress won out. "Oh, you *pobrecita*! Yes, go. And don't worry about waking up too soon. Joey and I will be just fine."

Back in her apartment six hours later Lainie felt completely rested. Before Rosa had gone home, she had reported that she had given Joey something for pain when he had awakened, but so far this afternoon he hadn't mentioned any discomfort.

Still, Lainie was worried about him. He seemed quiet, almost preoccupied. Rosa had made the couch out into a bed so that he could lie and watch the small TV that rested atop a brick and board bookcase. But instead of watching the TV, he was watching her.

"Joey, are you okay?" He nodded, but didn't say anything. Staring at him, she frowned. "I'm going to go take a shower and put on some fresh clothes. I won't be long. Do you need anything?" He shook his head.

Joey waited until he heard the shower start, then breathed a sigh of relief. At last he was alone! He had something terribly important to do, and it couldn't be done if other people were around. He looked at his arm. His cast presented a problem. He couldn't fold his hands together, but, he decided, under the circumstances maybe God wouldn't mind. He could still close his eyes real tight, and he did.

"Hi, God. It's me, Joey. I know this isn't the usual time I talk to you, but this is 'portant, and I don't want anyone to hear. You know my sister, Lainie? I've been thinking about somethin'. Rosa has Efrain to take care of her, and I have Lainie to take care of me, but she doesn't have anybody to take care of her. She cries at night when she thinks I'm asleep. She gets so tired. She has to sew all the time to make money for us, and she studies and studies so she can get a better job. So I've been thinking and I've decided she needs a husband!

"Yesterday I had to go to the hospital.' Joey tilted his head back toward the ceiling and squinted his eyes for a quick peep. "I'm real sorry I ran out in the street without looking. I promise I won't do it anymore. But anyway, there was someone really neat at the hospital. He's a doctor and everything! And the first time I woke up last night, he was here, but the second time I woke up, he was gone. Lainie said he had to leave and when I asked when he would be back, she said he wouldn't. Please have him come back real soon 'cause I like him." He thought for a minute. "And maybe have him ask her to go to dinner someplace. That would be real nice. She never gets to go anywhere. Amen."

When Lainie got out of the shower, she dried and powdered her body, then slipped into jade-green bikini briefs. The jeans she pulled up her legs and over her rounded hips had been washed so many times, they were as soft as fine kid. The faded orange top she pulled over her head and down around her rib cage to her waist fit with the familiarity of wear and the closeness of shrinkage. Then vigorously brushing her hair until it lay shining and loose down her back, she decided to devote the rest of the afternoon to Joey. She would sew later, after he went to bed. Walking into the living room, she was pleased to note that Joey looked much more cheerful.

About eight o'clock Lainie threw down her hand of Go Fish in disgust. "You're too good! You're a regular cardsharp. There's no way I'm playing another hand. Besides, it's time for bed."

"Aw, Lainie, not yet! Just one more hand."

"Not one more, young man. You need to get to sleep. You've done so well today, there's no reason why you can't go to school tomorrow."

"*School.* I'll let you win, I promise!"

"Joey!"

A knock interrupted their friendly argument, and Lainie, sitting cross-legged on the made-up couch, unwound her long legs and went to answer it.

"Rand!" Leaning against the door, he was supporting himself with one forearm against the jamb and was dressed casually in well-cut brown slacks and a gold pullover shirt. Although the colors looked wonderful on him, she got the impression that he was tired and wondered if he had come straight from the hospital.

To Rand Lainie looked like a vision, wearing jeans and a top that managed to mold every curve of her body. Her black hair spread over her shoulders; she wore no makeup; and her bare feet peeped out just below her jeans. He had never seen any woman look lovelier, and the most amazing thing to him was that he knew she wasn't even aware of it. Her eyes had lit up when she had first seen him, but then her lids had come down. When they raised again, there was only mild curiosity reflected in the jade depths of her gaze. He smiled because he was so glad to see her again. "I'm sorry I didn't call, but I was afraid you'd tell me not to come over."

"Rand!" Joey called with excitement.

Lainie jerked around to see Joey's face wearing the biggest grin she had seen on him all day.

Without waiting for an invitation, Rand stepped inside and closed the door. "Hi, buddy! You're looking a lot better than the last time I saw you."

Joey laughed happily. "I feel a lot better."

"Good. I'm glad to hear it." He sat down beside him. "How are you managing with your cast?"

"It's not too bad. Kyle and some of the guys came over today and signed it."

"So I see." Rand dutifully inspected the signatures.

"Would you sign it?" Joey asked eagerly.

"I'd be honored," he returned solemnly, and pulled out a pen.

Peering over Rand's shoulder and watching him sign his name, Lainie couldn't resist teasing. "You'll be able to tell which is Rand's signature, Joey, because it will be the only one you won't be able to read. To become a doctor you have to flunk penmanship."

"Is that why you didn't call last night?" Rand asked quietly. He finished and clicked his pen shut. "Because you couldn't read the phone number I wrote for you?"

Stiffening, she remembered that she hadn't thrown away his number as she had intended. Instead she had tucked it into a bureau drawer. "No. The reason I didn't call was because I didn't have any problems. Joey was fine."

Rand stood and faced her. "You could have called just to talk. It must have been lonely staying up all night by yourself."

Lonely, almost to the point of painfulness, Lainie thought. "Not at all," she denied.

Reaching out, he took possession of a silken handful of her black hair and whispered so that only she could hear. "Don't you ever get lonely at night?"

Lainie swallowed hard as a wave of warmth flushed her skin. She wanted to say *I never used to—not until I met you,* but she said nothing.

"Are you going to ask Lainie to go out to eat?" Joey asked loudly.

"Joey!" She looked from her brother to Rand. He smiled secretively at her, as if they shared some intimate joke.

"Yes, Joey, as a matter of fact, I am. Lainie, I hope you haven't eaten, because I really did come over to take you out to eat. I would have been here sooner, but I just couldn't break away from the hospital."

"No!" She shook her head as he tried again to take hold of her hair. She moved around him toward Joey. "I've eaten."

"Then come watch me eat."

"I can't leave." She gestured toward the made-up couch and her little brother.

"Get a baby-sitter. I'll pay."

"Yeah!" Joey exclaimed. "Rosa!"

"Hush, Joey." For the first time she wished she had taught him that children should be seen and not heard. "Rosa was here all morning. I can't ask her to come over again." Although she would be ecstatic to do so, Lainie added silently.

Rand shoved his hands in his pockets as a muscle contracted in his cheek. "There must be someone else. A teenage girl, perhaps?"

"There's—" Joey started.

"No one," Lainie snapped, then immediately regretted it after noticing the subdued expression on Joey's face. She turned to Rand. "Look, the bottom line is, I don't date."

"Never?"

"Never."

"Aw, Lainie—"

Rand interrupted Joey this time. "Why don't I help you into the bathroom, and you can brush your teeth? Then I can get you settled in bed like I did last night."

"You put me in bed last night?" This was obviously news to Joey.

"I sure did, with the pillows and everything. I even met Bunny Bear while you were sleeping."

"Wow!" Joey looked at Lainie. "Please go out to eat with him."

"Joey . . ." Lainie muttered warningly.

Joey had heard that warning tone before and knew when to back off. Sort of. He slipped off the couch and took Rand's hand. "Maybe she'll let you stay for a while anyway."

Curious emotions were assaulting Lainie as she watched the little boy lead Rand through the bedroom door. Joey genuinely liked him, and Rand seemed to like Joey. It had frequently worried her in the past that, other than Efrain, Joey had no male influence in his life. But then she would remind herself that he was a perfectly normal and happy child. And, in addition, they were doing wonderfully, just the two of them. They didn't need anyone else. Lainie grabbed the two pillows off the Hide-A-Bed and followed them.

A short time later Rand and Lainie were back in the living room, alone. Making sure that there was plenty of space between them, she swiveled to face him, ready to resist any new attempts to get her to go out.

"I like your hair that way."

Dammit! She hadn't expected that. Suddenly the space between them appeared to lessen. "Joey does too," she admitted, "so I try to wear it loose when I'm home. But I have to braid it for work. There's too much machinery there for it to get caught in."

"I don't even know what you do!" He was amazed with himself that he hadn't discovered something so important. But then maybe it wasn't so surprising, considering he had never before been so conscious of trying to do or say the right thing with a woman. In some ways he felt as awkward as a young boy.

She waved her hand toward the sewing machine, standing at the ready for the work she would do there tonight. "I sew in a garment factory." She waited for him to say something smart or derogatory about her job. He said neither.

"Really? And do you like it?"

"Like it?" He sounded genuinely interested, and suddenly she felt thrown off balance. "I like the people who work there. And as for the job . . . I'm used to it. I've done it for four years now."

"Is there something else you'd rather do?"

Part of her hair had feathered forward, and she tossed it back over her shoulder with a flick of her hand. "I'm studying education. I want to be a teacher."

Nodding seriously, he sat down. "Education is a marvelous field. We need all the good teachers we can get. What kind of teacher are you studying to be?"

"Spanish." Since he had the chair, she chose the edge of the sofa's mattress to perch on. "Years ago, as a young girl newly arrived from Mexico, Rosa came to work as my family's housekeeper. When I was born, she still spoke more Spanish than English, so I grew up with Spanish as a second language. I studied it in high school too, and enjoyed it enough that I decided to pursue it in college. After I got my high school diploma, that is."

"How do you manage with your work and all?"

She shrugged. "I go to school at night. Except this semester they weren't offering the courses at night that I needed, so I'm waiting until the summer semester." Unconsciously she sighed. "Since I can take just one or two courses a semester, it's going to take a long time."

"I'm impressed. Really and truly impressed."

She didn't want his admiration, she told herself.

She didn't want his interest. And she especially didn't want him looking at her as if he wanted to take her in his arms and kiss her until she couldn't think straight. A coolness frosted her words. "Don't be."

"Why?"

He certainly asked *why* a lot, she reflected without humor. "Because I'm doing nothing more or less than a lot of other single mothers do every day around this country."

"Maybe, but I'm not sitting in their living room. I'm sitting in yours, and I'm still impressed."

She cursed silently as a warmth curled its way into her stomach. It wasn't fair. She couldn't claim vulnerability as she had last night, and he was *still* affecting her!

"Why don't you date?"

The question caught her unawares. "Because I don't want to," she said through clenched teeth, "and before you ask *why*, let me tell you that it's none of your business!"

He regarded her thoughtfully. "What is it, Lainie? Why are you fighting me so hard?"

She started to deny it, then decided it would be no use. "I don't seem to be fighting you hard enough. Last night I asked you why you were here. You kissed me, and—"

"You kissed me back."

"Yes, I did. But then I told you, I'm not looking for a lover." Watching him as closely as she was, she couldn't help but see the golden brown of his eyes darken as she said the word *lover*.

His voice had a husky quality to it when next he

spoke. "I can't deny that I want to make love to you, Lainie, but believe it or not, that's not all I want."

In spite of her good intentions her pulse rate quickened. "It doesn't matter. Don't you see? Whatever it is you want, you want too much. Involvement is out of the question. I just can't."

Something hurtful tightened in his gut. He could hardly bear to ask the question. "Is there someone else?"

"No, no." She shook her head, causing her hair, as it swung back and forth, to pick up the light from a nearby lamp. "It's not that. It's something down deep inside me that I'm not even sure I can explain to myself, let alone to you."

"Try."

"Rand, you're a man who's very much used to having his own way. I'm a woman who will never be able to let a man dominate her. We're misfits."

His forehead creased uncomprehendingly. "What makes you think I would try to dominate you?"

Her mouth twisted ruefully. "Those people at the hospital all but bowed and scraped to you."

He leaned forward earnestly. "That's at my work. It has nothing to do with my personal life."

"You don't even realize the effect you have on people, Rand."

"You might give me a chance, Lainie, without condemning me out of hand. What have you got to lose?"

She jumped to her feet. "I have to consider Joey. There's the danger that he will grow too fond of you."

He stood too. "So Joey gains a new friend and so do I. Where's the harm in that?"

"I . . ." She pushed her fingers through her hair, held it for a moment, then let the hair fall back into place. She knew her reasons were good ones. It was just that when she voiced them aloud to Rand, they suddenly seemed to lack importance.

With the gentlest of pressures his hands closed over her arms. "Lainie, there's no need to react so defensively. I would never do anything to hurt either you or Joey."

"Why do I want to believe you so badly?" she asked slowly.

He pulled her toward him until the tips of her breasts were pressed against his chest. "Because you know I wouldn't lie to you."

"Then tell me," she requested, despair tingeing her tone, "how I know that, tonight, when you've finally gone, I'll regret what's about to happen?"

"I don't think you will."

She saw his head lower. She felt his arms close around her. She knew that he was going to kiss her. But still, she wasn't prepared.

His mouth touched hers ever so lightly as he began to sample the sweetness of her lips. A bite here, a nibble there, a taste everywhere. She swayed into him and opened her mouth to his. His tongue dipped, coaxing a response, increasing the intimacy. Her hands slowly crept around his back, and she could feel his muscles ripple beneath her palms as he shifted to draw her nearer. Desire unfurled and passion took hold of her mind as heat began to build deep inside her body.

He had never thought that just the kiss of a

woman's lips could make him feel this hard-biting need. She had a sweetness in her that seemed to flow slowly, thickly, like heated honey, into his bloodstream. He groaned. Dammit! Why couldn't he go slow? With her his need was wildly immediate. His hands crushed into the fine silk of her hair. He was used to having his way with women, and he wanted all of Lainie.

He knew if he continued the kiss, he wouldn't be able to stop and he would have her. That would be heaven. But he also knew that if he allowed the lovemaking to happen, he would lose her. And that would be a hell that might never stop. Gradually he relaxed his hold on her and withdrew his lips from hers.

He shut his eyes for a moment and took several deep breaths of air. Resting his wrists on her shoulders, he clasped his hands together over her hair at the back of her neck. Not until he felt his control returning did he open his eyes and look at her. "If I were to ask you very politely, then would you have dinner with me tomorrow night?"

Unable to speak, she started to shake her head, but he stopped her by putting his thumbs on either side of her neck.

"Think about it before you say no."

"Rand—"

"I'm only asking you to come to dinner, Lainie, not share my bed. You can set the limits for the evening. I'll even arrange for a baby-sitter. There're plenty of Candy Stripers at the hospital who would love to do it. And tomorrow night is Friday night."

"I work on Saturday mornings."

"So do I, but I still want to go out with you Friday night."

How she could say it, she didn't know. But she did, very softly, very clearly: "No."

He held her gaze for a minute, and her firm expression did not waver. But deep within the jade recesses of her eyes, he thought he caught a glimmer of vulnerability. It was that which made him murmur, "All right, Lainie." He left, closing the door behind him.

Her legs gave out, and Lainie sank onto the couch. As that wild teenager she had once been, she had kissed plenty of boys. She had even made love with one she was fond of and who had been mad for her. She had been so disappointed that she had never seen the need to repeat the "process." But now, after having practically drowned in the passion of Rand's kiss, she knew with unquestioning certainty that, if she were to become his lover, he would never disappoint her.

If. Dear Lord! It had come down to *if.*

Four

Late that night, as Joey and Lainie lay sleeping in their small apartment, Rand sat at the desk in the book-lined study of his home in the exclusive River Oaks suburb of Houston.

The house and all that it held represented materially what he had accomplished so far in his life. The actual amount of money it stood for was negligible to him. What was important was that he had earned it himself, without using his family's money, and that while he was earning it, he had done a lot of good along the way.

He remembered Lainie's apartment with the homemade curtains and the photographs of the people she loved and the sense of home he had known there.

Rand had never much thought about having a real home, with a wife and a family, until Alex had found his Rachel. That was just over a year ago. Then shortly afterward, deep in the wild jungles of Montaraz, Rand had been kidnapped and held captive in a miserable little shack. Realizing his life might end at any moment, he had done some reevaluating.

He knew he had already accomplished more than most men do in a lifetime. With the exception of the period when, fresh out of college, he and Alex had been in Montaraz, he had devoted his life to helping other people. Hell, even during that short time he had thought, however foolishly, he was helping people. But still, he had decided that there was something missing, and he had vowed to try to find it.

And then Alex had showed up, and together they had blazed their way out of that hellhole. When they had gotten back, Rachel had laid down the law. Rand would never return to Montaraz again on one of his mercy missions and that was that. She didn't want either Rand or Alex risking their lives anymore. And she had proceeded to make Rand godfather to the most precious little girl he had ever seen.

It was then that he had known what was missing from his life. He, too, wanted a wife who would worry about him, and a son or a daughter to raise.

His gaze scanned the study. One of the top designers in Houston had decorated and furnished the place. It was a beautiful house, but Lainie could make it a home. He was sure of that. And not with just her talents as a homemaker either, but with her presence. He wanted to see her here with him.

Suddenly a big grin creased his face, and he leaned over and picked up the phone. After punching out a series of numbers, he waited.

"Hello." It was the sleepy voice of Alex.

"Wake up. I've got something to tell you."

"Rand?" Instantly all traces of Alex's grogginess vanished. "What's wrong?"

"Nothing's wrong. Well, actually, at the moment, everything's not entirely right. But in reality nothing's wrong. Although things could certainly be better."

"Rand, did you call me up at"—there was a pause, and Rand pictured Alex squinting at the clock—"two o'clock in the morning to tell me you've lost your mind? Because if that's all—"

"Give me that phone," he heard Rachel say. "Rand, what's wrong? Are you sick?"

"No, love. I've never felt better. Actually I just wanted you two to know that I've found the woman I'm going to marry."

"You did? Rand, that's great! Who is she? When can we meet her? Wait! When's the wedding?"

"Well, that's the problem, Rachel. At the moment she won't even accept a dinner invitation from me."

"What? Are you sure?"

He laughed. "I'm afraid so. But don't worry. I'm not giving up. It's just going to take a little time, that's all."

"You go easy with her, you hear?" Rachel advised sternly. "Don't scare her away."

"Rand?" Alex was back on the phone. "I gather congratulations would be a bit premature."

"A bit."

"Now, you listen to me. Rachel and I have waited long enough for you to find the right woman. Don't screw it up!"

"Thanks for the confidence, friend. Go back to sleep. I'll let you know when the wedding is going to be."

"Good night. Oh, and Rand?"

"Yes?"

"Next time call during the day. I'm a father now. I panic easily."

"Right."

Friday came and went, and Lainie didn't hear a word from Rand. But then what had she expected? she asked herself. She had said no to his invitation, and a man like Rand Bennett wouldn't react lightly to being turned down.

She worked Saturday morning at the garment factory, and as usual took the afternoon for cleaning and shopping. Ordinarily by Saturday night she was exhausted and collapsed in front of the TV with Joey. Not tonight though. She was running on nervous energy she hadn't known she had.

She glanced at Joey. Something was wrong, although she couldn't quite put her finger on what it might be. Perhaps his arm was bothering him. He had said it wasn't, but he was showing only a desultory interest in his collection of Hot Wheels. They surrounded him on the couch that was still made out into a bed, and they usually had the capacity to hold him enthralled for hours.

"Joey, I was thinking of doing some sewing.

Would you mind if I put the TV in your room? You could get on your bed and watch it."

He raised his blue eyes to her, a troubled expression etched on his young face. "How come Rand hasn't called you?"

She groaned inwardly. Not Joey too! She really didn't need it from him. Not after the several scoldings she had already received from Rosa.

"Honey, I told him I didn't want to go out to dinner with him. A man like Rand doesn't ask twice."

"But you weren't supposed to say no!"

"What?" A knock sounded at the front door. "What do you mean, I wasn't supposed to say no?" There was another knock. "Oh, drat! Just a minute, Joey. Let me see who's at the door and then I'll be right back." Still bothered by his reaction, she went to the door and jerked it open. It was Rand. He wore a blue V-neck T-shirt and beige pleated linen slacks and looked handsomer than she would have thought any man could.

"I would have called, but—" He shrugged, then gave her an innocent smile that caused her heart to lurch. Before she could respond, however, he caught sight of Joey behind her back and proceeded to walk around her. "Well, at least someone's glad to see me."

The little boy had a grin pasted ear to ear. "I knew you'd come!" Joey exclaimed. "I just knew you would."

"You did?" Rand went down on his haunches in front of the boy. "Well, then you obviously knew more than your sister."

"That's 'cause she doesn't know what I know."

"Ah, a wise young man. Well, then maybe you

can tell me, if I ask Lainie out for dinner tonight, will she go?"

Joey nodded vigorously. "Yup."

Rand stood and faced Lainie. "You heard it here first. According to your very own resident sage, you're going to accept my invitation."

Lainie was torn between exasperation and amusement. The rapid beat of her pulse, Rand's inherent charm, and Joey's eager expression were almost an unbeatable combination. Still, she felt it would be wiser to say no. "I'm sorry, Rand, but—"

"You haven't heard the options yet. First of all, I've got an extremely nice young lady waiting in the car, and she's very eager to sit with Joey while we go out."

"You brought a baby-sitter?"

"But if that doesn't appeal to you, I'll run her home, buy a couple of steaks, and prepare us a meal here."

"You'd cook?"

"Actually I'm not bad."

"I suppose I should have known."

"Who did you bring, Rand?" Joey asked excitedly. "What's her name?"

"Her name's Donna, she's sixteen, and she's very pretty. I can almost guarantee that you'll like her. She volunteers her spare time with the kids in the pediatric unit at the hospital. And guess what?"

"What?"

"She *loves* to play cars."

"Oh, please, Lainie. Can she come in?"

Angrily she folded her arms across her chest and glared at Rand. "This is not fair, and you know it. You're being your usual overpowering self."

His eyes stayed on her as he requested, "Joey, would you go in your room for just a few minutes?"

"But—"

"Now, please?"

Joey left the room. Seconds stretched between them, along with something else that Lainie knew had nothing to do with either the dinner invitation, or the baby-sitter waiting in the car, or Joey in the next room. It was a feeling that had only to do with the two of them. She was just beginning to get a glimmer of the potential power of it, and it frightened her to death.

"Lainie," he said softly, "you're right. I am being overpowering, even when I know I shouldn't be."

"That's a neat trick you have of confessing your faults. I'm sure it has the desired effect with other people." She took a step, intending to move away from him, but he caught her arm with his hand, holding her so that the length of her side lightly touched his.

"There are no tricks involved, Lainie. With you there is only honesty. You've got me running scared."

"I don't understand." She shrugged out of his grasp. She had to.

"Yes, you do." His voice was as soft as a gloved hand stroking her skin and had the same effect. "I set all this up because I was afraid you'd refuse to come with me. I was hoping that if I took care of all of your objections beforehand, you wouldn't be able to turn me down."

Searching his golden brown eyes, Lainie found only sincerity, and she began to weaken. She realized that she was guilty of what she had accused him of doing—lying—because his confession and his honesty did indeed affect her. Much more than she could adequately deal with.

With an impatient gesture he raked his hair off his forehead, yet there was no trace of that impatience in his voice as he spoke to her. "I said it before, and I'll say it again. I don't mean you any harm. Believe it, Lainie." He smiled gently. "Look, you won't even have to change clothes. I know this smoky little jazz bistro where jeans and sandals are the order of the day."

Her eyes lowered uncertainly to her jeans. Although she never gave much thought to it, jeans and knit tops made up the major portion of her wardrobe. These particular jeans were so old and faded, she couldn't even remember the year she had bought them. "Are you sure?"

"Absolutely, and they have the best pasta in town. How does that sound?"

"Good," she admitted reluctantly. Unfortunately Rand didn't seem to understand the word *no;* and what was more, she was finding it harder and harder to say no to him. Realizing that she was about to make a decision that she probably shouldn't, she began to rationalize. It had been so long since she had been out for an evening of relaxation and entertainment, she reminded herself. What could one dinner hurt? The rationalization, flimsy as it was, eased her mind somewhat. "Oh, all right."

The bistro was just as he described, and the pasta and the music were equally hot. By her second glass of wine Lainie found she was relaxed and enjoying herself. Occasionally she would catch someone looking their way, obviously recognizing Rand, but no one was obtrusive. "You know, I tend to forget that you're a famous doctor."

"Good. That's exactly what I want."

"You don't like being famous?"

"Not when it interferes with my work—or a night out with someone I'm trying to impress."

The thought of Rand having to try to impress anyone was absolutely ludicrous to her, and she dismissed it with a toss of her head. "You must be very proud of the work you do."

"Yes, I am." He took a swallow of his wine, then carefully set down the glass, taking extra time to place it just so. "Lainie . . . have you ever heard my name being linked with the country of Montaraz?"

"Yes," she said slowly. "Just last year. Your name was in the headlines here and probably around the world. You were kidnapped while trying to get medical supplies to needy villagers. When your friend brought you back to Houston, the media made a great fuss over you. They called you a hero."

His mouth twisted wryly. "The media has always had a tendency to romanticize the worst times of my life."

"I don't understand. You were down there trying to help those people, weren't you?"

"Oh, yes. I used to go down there on a regular basis. They got that part right at any rate. But in the last few years, the media has conveniently forgotten to mention why I was so at home in Montaraz; why I knew those people and the terrain of the country so well; even how I was able to get into the country in the first place; and then how Alex and I were able to get out." He drew in a deep breath and intently fixed his gaze on her face. "I was a mercenary, Lainie." He waited the space of two heartbeats. She didn't say anything, and he continued. "When Alex and I graduated from college, we decided we wanted to do something meaningful, something to help the world. Idealistically and quite wrongly we decided that we could single-handedly save this little country in Central America that, at the time, was fighting for its life. We grew up fast."

Lainie remained absolutely silent, giving him no clue as to what was going on behind those jade-green eyes of hers. He had to find out. "Well?" he demanded.

"What do you expect me to say, Rand? I can tell that place and time holds painful memories for you. I get the impression you don't even like to talk about it."

"I *never* talk about it." Rand stared down into his wineglass for a moment. She wasn't reacting as he had expected, but he couldn't leave it alone. "I want to make absolutely sure you understand, Lainie. I was a cold-blooded mercenary. Aren't you shocked?"

"No. I'm sorry, Rand, but I'm not. I really haven't known you all that long, but there is one thing that I'm absolutely certain of. The concern you have for people is very real. It's deep in your bones. It didn't just grow there overnight. You were born that way. It's the way your genes are arranged. Your idealism may have led to disillusionment, so that you went astray for a while, but I can see quite clearly the man you are today. I would never believe that you were a cold-blooded anything."

Because of the nature of his profession Rand strove to maintain objectivity in all things. He wasn't touched easily. But he had never heard anything that moved him quite the way Lainie's words did. He wanted to tell her that she was the most beautiful woman he had ever known, both inside and out. He wanted to take her into his arms and hold her until she understood the strength of his feelings for her. Instead, he said simply, "I wanted to make sure you knew."

"Why?"

"Because openness and honesty are important . . . between two people who—"

"Rand." She held up her hand, stopping him. "I don't know what you were going to say, but perhaps its better if you don't say it."

He looked at her for a minute. "I'm going too fast, aren't I? It's a fault of mine."

"This is indeed an extraordinary night," she commented lightly. "Earlier you confessed to being overpowering, and now you're confessing another fault!"

He chuckled, reached over, and took her hand. It fit perfectly into his, he thought. "How about I just say, openness and honesty are important between two people who . . . like each other . . . a lot."

Lainie threw back her head and laughed. Despite the undercurrent of sexual tension that seemed to run through their relationship, despite his self-confessed faults, she realized that she actually did like him.

"Well, what do you think?" he asked, enjoying

the sound of her laughter. "Can you live with that scenario?"

"I can live with it, Doctor."

"Good. Because, lady, I sure do *like* you—a lot—and I'm about to make a suggestion."

"A suggestion?" she asked. His fingers were rubbing across the back of her hand, bringing up the tiny hairs that grew there, sending tingles of warmth skidding up her arm. "In our short relationship suggestions from you have been few and far between."

"Then you'll be glad to know that I'm about to turn over a new leaf. And here it is. I promise that I will try—"

"Try?" She was getting used to his touch, and she didn't know if that was good or bad.

"To always call first before coming over to your home."

His hands were so beautiful, so strong, yet she was finding out that they could also be quite gentle. "You left something out."

One brow arched, as if to say he found it impossible to believe that he could have left anything out. "What?"

"That once you called, you would come over only if I agreed."

"Well, of course. That goes without saying."

"And in fact, *has* quite frequently in our short past." In spite of herself she was beginning to find his unconscious arrogance funny, even endearing.

He ignored her pointed barb. "At any rate I would like to take you and Joey on a picnic tomorrow. I know a great spot."

Reluctantly she withdrew her hand from his. "I

don't think so, Rand. Dinner tonight is enough, at least for now."

"What do you and Joey usually do on Sundays?" he demanded, scowling briefly. "You don't work, do you?"

"No. Rosa takes Joey to church in the mornings to give me a chance to rest. Then Sunday afternoons I try to plan things that Joey will like and that we can do together. I don't have a car, so we're sort of limited. But the buses run to the museums and parks, and on nice days we sometimes take a bus all the way to Galveston."

"Do you ever have picnics?"

"Yes," she admitted.

"Well?" The one brow of his that she was coming to know so well arched again.

"You're a perfectly rotten human being, did you know that? You always have to get your way."

He adopted a wounded look. "And after all the nice things you just said about me! Besides, I told you: I've turned over a new leaf. And by the way I'll take care of the food. You won't have to do a thing. What time would be good for you?"

She sighed wearily. "One o'clock will be fine."

"Now, Joey, I want to explain something to you before Rand gets here." She tugged at the neckline of the forest-green knit top she had put on an hour earlier. It was nicer than the tops she usually wore, but the cowl neckline was also a bit lower than what she was used to wearing. She glanced at Joey. One of his favorite tunes was being played on the radio, and he was dancing around the living room. "Will you be still? I'm trying to talk to you."

"What?" Joey could barely contain his excitement over the three of them going on a picnic.

Lainie strolled across the room and clicked the radio off. "Come over here and sit on the couch with me."

"When's Rand going to get here?"

"In just a few minutes, okay?" She waited until he was relatively settled beside her. "Now this is what I want to say to you. We're going on this picnic today with Rand, but I want you to understand that it doesn't mean anything. He's a friend, that's all, sort of like Kyle is a friend."

"Kyle?" Joey thought about it for a minute. "That's good. Kyle is my best friend. We help each other and take care of each other."

Lainie slumped. This wasn't going well. Her main concern was that Joey would become too attached to Rand. She was afraid that when Rand stopped showering the two of them with his attention—as he surely would—Joey would be terribly hurt. She wouldn't allow herself to admit that she also might be hurt. "Maybe what I should have said was that we haven't known Rand very long. Just because we're going out with him today doesn't mean we'll even see him again. It's true he's a friend, but not as *good* a friend as Kyle is, because you've known Kyle longer and—" She paused for a breath, pretty sure that she was going in circles and not saying at all what she should.

Joey shook his head. "It didn't take long at all for Kyle and me to become best friends." Impulsively he reached over and hugged her. "You'll see. Everything is going to be all right." A knock at the door had him jumping down off the couch and racing to the door. "Hi, Rand!"

"Hi, buddy. Are you ready to have some fun?"

"Are you sure this picnic spot you've been talking about is worth all this?" Lainie asked Rand as she stood on his shoulder and prepared to lever herself up onto a brick wall he had assured her they needed to scale.

"Absolutely! Joey, quit giggling. Your sister is doing just fine. That's right, Lainie. Just sit on top of the wall and don't move. I'll be right there to help you."

"But what about Joey? He has a cast. Shouldn't you hand him up to me? How can he possibly . . . ?" She looked over her shoulder to where Rand and Joey had been standing only moments before. No one was there. "Rand? Joey? Where are you?"

"Right here, Lainie."

She twisted forward again, and there, ten feet below her on the ground was Joey, jumping up and down, whooping with glee. Rand was right beside him. He held out his arms. "Jump. I'll catch you."

"How did you get there?" she demanded.

"There's a gate a few feet down the wall. Joey and I decided to use it."

"Rand Bennett! When I get my hands on you . . . !" She slid off the top of the wall and into his arms. Rand caught her easily, but deliberately let his knees buckle, and they both went tumbling onto the ground. Joey went into gales of laughter.

Laughing herself, Lainie lightly hit Rand's arm. "I thought you said you'd catch me!"

"I did catch you!" he protested. "But I didn't say I wouldn't fall doing it."

"Somehow, in some way, I will get you for this," she promised ominously.

His golden-brown eyes were shining into hers with such intensity, Lainie decided it was rather like looking directly into the sun. The effect was somewhat blinding.

"You can have me," he said softly, "anytime you want me."

"Kiss her, Rand. Kiss her."

"Joey!" Lainie scrambled to her feet, embarrassed.

Rand came to his feet more slowly. "All in good time, Joey. All in good time." He rubbed his hands together. "Now, let's see if we can find that picnic basket I put someplace around here."

Lainie slowly turned in a circle, taking in the beautiful wooded park and meticulously landscaped garden. Walkways that ambled seemingly at random had thickly planted borders of dahlias, periwinkles, snapdragons, and freesia. Around a lush green lawn, clouds of daffodils and thickets of narcissus stretched uninterrupted. Statuary appeared here and there. And as a backdrop for the tumultuous jumble of color, tall, stately oaks stood, trailing their gray lace streamers of moss in the breeze. "Rand, should we be here? This is beautiful, but it also looks very private."

"It is, but it's okay. I know the owner."

She looked at him suspiciously. "How well?"

"Very, as it happens. You might say we are on the most intimate of terms."

"Uh-huh. This is your place, isn't it?"

"You live in a park, Rand?" Joey asked, amazed.

Rand grinned and pointed. "I live in a house that is just through those trees over there. We could have gotten here by entering the front door and coming through the house, but I thought this might be more fun."

"You're dangerous," Lainie murmured, shaking her head.

"I'll go see if I can find the basket," Joey announced and took off.

"Good idea." Rand turned to Lainie and pulled her to him. "Did you get scraped or bruised anyplace when you fell?" He began running his hands up her arms and around to her back, then slipped his hand under her top. "I'd be glad to kiss it and make it better."

"You may not be aware of it, Doctor," she said breathlessly, as his hands continued to roam intimately over her skin, coming so close, but never quite touching her breasts, "but modern medicine has advanced way beyond that particular technique."

"What a shame," he whispered huskily, then pressed his lips to her neck. "I've always been most fond of kissing things better." She felt his teeth nibble a sensitive path down the length of her neck, then his lips, tenderly kissing their way back up. "See?"

"You've made your point." A weakness slowly wound its way into her limbs.

"Not yet." And his lips lowered to hers.

In the short time that they had known one another, Rand had gradually accustomed her to his kisses and his touches so that she no longer shied away from them or felt them strange. In fact, their mouths seemed to be made for each other, adapting perfectly to the other's shape. And the way his hands moved over her skin could shatter her composure in an instant, reminding her that she was very much a woman with all the physical needs and wants that a woman has. Her arms crept around his neck as the kiss deepened.

"I found the basket!" Joey called excitedly. "Hey, guys, come on! It was under a tree."

"We'll continue this later," Rand promised huskily.

The English wicker picnic basket that Joey had discovered was like Aladdin's lamp. Everything that one could wish for was in it. Besides a huge throw of beige cashmere that Rand casually spread over the grass, there were three complete sets of china and crystal. And then came the food. For Joey there were fried drumsticks, potato salad, deviled eggs, orange sections, and a thermos of cold milk. When Joey saw the milk, he protested. "Aw, I was hoping I could have a soda. I don't get to drink them very often."

"Milk is better for you," Rand said firmly. "But if you eat everything on your plate, look what you can have for dessert." He reached into the basket and came back out with a piece of two-layered chocolate cake.

"Oooh, look, Lainie!"

"I assume that chocolate cake has the recommended daily allowance of vitamins and minerals?" she asked dryly.

"Uh, Lainie, why don't you fix Joey's plate while I set out our food?"

"This isn't our food?"

"I thought we should have something a little different." His hand began to dip into the basket and reappeared with all sorts of wondrous things.

There were thinly sliced pieces of rare roast beef that had been carefully rolled around cold asparagus tips, plus a bowl of peeled cherry tomatoes marinating in a dressing of oil, vinegar, and herbs. There was a pinwheel of soft white cheese stuffed with green herbs and small loaves of French bread to spread it on. And to top it off succulent peaches and a chilled bottle of white wine.

There was no more talking as the three of them proceeded to eat everything in sight.

Some time later, while Joey was finishing his piece of chocolate cake, Lainie lay back on the soft throw and stared up at the sky. It was a perfect day, she mused. A day to be remembered, because perfect days didn't come along that often. And she would enjoy today to the fullest, she determined, because the fact was, no matter how hard she tried to deny it, she would be hurt when Rand stopped coming around.

Although her life was hard, she had never thought to complain. The hours of her days were so busy, they overflowed. She had believed she was thoroughly satisfied, complete. Then Rand had come along, filling up empty spaces within her that she hadn't even known were empty. When he left, her life would return to the way it had been, with one exception. Now she would know where all the empty places were. She closed her eyes and heard Rand speaking to Joey.

"If you walk down that path over there, it will lead you to a pool where the gardener has some fancy fish called *koi*. They're imperial carp that are descended from fish that were originally owned by the emperor of Japan."

"Really?"

"I told the gardener to leave out a pail of their food for you to feed them. Just throw in a few pieces at a time. They'll come right up to the edge of the water."

"Wow!"

Opening her eyes, Lainie was just in time to see Joey all but break his other arm in his haste to race down the path and investigate the phenomenon Rand had described to him.

She came up on one elbow. "Very sneaky."

"Thank you." He made an effort at bowing from a sitting position and did a credible job. "Would you like one of these peaches?"

She nodded, lazily pushing her unbound hair back over her shoulder.

He picked up one of the peaches and studied it thoughtfully. "Would you like to hear my theory on Adam and Eve?"

"I'm not sure. It's probably totally mad."

"Please! I have all sorts of degrees in the sciences. All of my theories make absolute sense."

"Okay." She sighed good-naturedly. "Let's hear it."

"Ah, good. I was hoping you would ask. Well, it's just this. I can't believe that Adam was ever tempted by an apple."

"No?"

"No. An apple is much too neat and tidy. I mean, you bite into an apple and what happens?"

"Why don't you tell me."

"It *crunches*. And there's nothing remotely sexy about crunching."

"Sexy?"

"Of course. Now, you take a peach." The shift of his voice as it went from lighthearted to deep and sensuous was so smooth, it almost went unnoticed by Lainie. Almost, that is, until it registered with her exactly what it was he was saying. "A peach has skin that is as soft and downy as that of the most intimate and delicate of human skin." She swallowed hard. "And even before you taste it, you can smell the rich scent of it. The moment the mouth touches it, the senses are assaulted. As your teeth gently penetrate the flesh of the fruit, you receive a tiny explosion of the essence of the flavor and the sweet juices."

He slowly raised his eyes from the contemplation of the peach in his hand and deliberately bit into the fruit. A small trickle of the juice escaped his mouth and ran down his chin. "It's rather like making love—a little messy, but *very* enjoyable." He smiled and held the peach out to her. "Take a bite and see for yourself."

Lainie was trembling and a mist of desire had descended around her, blocking out the perfect day, the beautiful park, and the exquisite gardens. The desire blocked out everything but its focus: Rand, who seemed to have moved closer to her.

"Come on, Lainie," he whispered, "don't be

afraid. Open your mouth and let yourself taste the sweetness."

Blindly she opened her mouth to receive a portion of the fruit between her teeth, and when she did bite down, she experienced everything that he had just described, even to the tiny trickle of its nectar down her chin.

He came down beside her and began licking the golden liquid from her chin, until her elbow gave way, and she fell the short distance to her back. Rand followed. "Now me, Lainie. I want to feel your tongue on me."

Of its own accord her tongue drew in the wetness that had lingered on his chin. It was a combination of the taste of his skin and the flavorful peach. His chin felt rough under her tongue, but then she ventured to the smoothness of his lips. And when they parted, she lifted her head from the ground so that her tongue could seek and find the wondrous sweetness she knew would be within.

Rand was on fire, but he fought for control. His fingers delved into her hair to cradle her head and slowly lower her back to the ground. He kept his mouth open so that she could have unrestricted access, but when she at last gave a little cry and began nipping at his lips, he could take it no longer. He ground his mouth into hers, giving full vent to the heat blazing inside him.

Lainie had never wanted someone like this before. It was almost unbearable. One of Rand's legs lay between hers, and with it, he began exerting pressure against that vulnerable point between her thighs that was covered by only the soft denim of her jeans. His hand slid under her top and closed around a breast. Something contracted in her stomach, hard and hot.

His lean, muscled body was half covering her, his leg was pressing up against her, his fingers were stroking the bare flesh of her breast, and his tongue was mating each time it thrust in and out of her mouth. She was being possessed by him. There was only one more act that would make it more complete, and she strained against him, wordlessly begging him to take that one other step that would completely block out the day and the sun and bring them both to a place of sweet, dark oblivion.

He drug his mouth off hers and groaned, "God, we have to stop!" Pain made his voice rough and uneven. "We can't go on, we can't. But I have to taste you, to pull the nectar you have inside you into me, just for a little while." He pushed up her top until her breasts were exposed, and then his mouth fastened on one tightly erect nipple and began to suck. At that point the sun and the day did disappear for Lainie, and unknown to her, tears began to slide down her face. Rand was a power that she could no longer fight, and her body craved everything he was offering.

She felt his mouth leave her nipple and waited impatiently for him to transfer his attention to the other one. He did. But it was with a gentler motion that he pulled it into his mouth, and then, after only what seemed like a moment, he released it and carefully drew her top over her breasts. Slowly he shifted until he was lying beside her, with the long length of his body barely touching her.

Lainie felt his departure. She tried to move, but

found it impossible. None of her muscles worked, and somewhere deep inside her she was hurting. She didn't know what to do about it. There was no rhyme or reason to what had just happened. She knew that, and she still wanted him.

As the heaving of his chest lessened, Rand turned to her and saw the tears staining her cheeks. Tenderly he slid his arm underneath her shoulders and raised himself on his elbow so that he could look down into her face. Unblinking tear-washed jade eyes returned his gaze.

Slowly, carefully, he brushed away her tears. "If it weren't for Joey, I would have made love to you, you know that, don't you?"

She nodded.

"You're used to being in total control of a situation. Unfortunately so am I. But it's going to be okay, because we can handle this together."

"I'm not sure. I'm not even sure we should try."

"I am. I've never been surer of anything in my entire life."

He was such a remarkable man, she thought, looking into his golden-brown eyes. There were so many facets to him. He was a kind, compassionate man, but he was also funny and infuriating and brilliant. And only minutes ago, if circumstances had been different, she would have made love with him. "I guess we'd better go find Joey."

"I guess we'd better," he agreed with a smile.

Five

"But this is an exception!" Rand protested, using that half-angel, half-devil smile of his that told her he knew he was once again doing things all wrong, but begging her to forgive him.

Lainie tried not to be persuaded. "You told me you'd start calling before you came over."

"And I have. Come on, admit it. I've been very good this past week, haven't I?"

"It's true. You've called every night, and after being perfectly outrageous, you've managed to finagle an invitation to come over two nights out of seven."

"Not a very good average, is it?"

"Rand, how can I make you understand? I can't see you every night, even if I wanted to."

His voice lowered, and his eyes warmed. "Do you want to?"

It didn't matter that he could alter her heart rate with just a change of the register of his voice, she told herself. She had to remain firm. "I bring sewing home with me to make extra money. If I don't get it done, I don't make the money."

The laugh lines on his face disappeared. "I wish it weren't that way."

"Well, it is."

He sighed and combed his fingers through his hair. "Okay. Look, the reason I came over is because I wanted to issue an invitation to you in person."

"An invitation? What kind?"

"An important one—at least to me. And I didn't want you to say no."

The first thing that jumped into her head was that he was once again trying to ride roughshod over her, but one thing stopped her. He had said the invitation was important to him. The least she could do was hear it. "What is it?"

"Next weekend there's going to be a ball, a charity ball."

Her heart sank. How could he expect her to accept such an invitation? Didn't he realize that he should not have even considered asking her?

He saw the closed expression on her face and rushed on. "I know that this is something of a last-minute invitation, considering the magnitude of the event, but to tell you the truth, I've been trying to think of ways to get you to say yes."

She shook her head. "Rand, I can't go."

"Don't say no right away. Take time to think about it."

Think about it! What in the world was there to

think about? she wondered. Was she supposed to think about how women like herself, women who had ordinary jobs and led ordinary lives, never got to go to grand functions like the one he was talking about? Or maybe she was supposed to think about how she absolutely hated the thought of Rand going with any other woman but herself? Her voice began rising, revealing her distress. "Why did you even ask me?"

"Because, Lainie, I want you to go with me so badly."

She threw up her hands. "You're impossible! And so is your hope that I'll go to a—a charity ball with you."

"Lainie." The tender way he said her name almost stopped her heart. "Please listen to me."

She felt her eyes moisten with tears and blinked them away. Why did he keep pushing the issue? Didn't he know how much she would love to go with him? She wished with all her heart that she had the means to buy a gown that would take his breath away and make him proud that she was on his arm, but it was an impossible dream. Life had laid out different paths for the two of them, and this was a perfect example of why their individual paths should continue separately.

"This is for the American Heart Association. I'm almost obligated to attend, but I don't want to go without you. I won't. Now, I've thought about this, and I realize that you're probably reluctant to go because you feel you don't have anything to wear."

"You figured that out all by yourself, did you?"

He ignored her sarcasm, spoken barely above a whisper. "Let me buy you a dress." Her head jerked up and her eyes showed the shock she felt at his suggestion. Because Rand couldn't take the alienation he saw there, he reached for her. But, too fast, she stepped away. "Lainie, forget your pride this one time. Let me do it. I can't think of anything I would enjoy spending my money on more."

"You can take your money and—"

This time he was faster than she was. He pulled her into his arms and held her tightly against him. "All right, all right. I'll drop the subject for now. But, Lainie, there's got to be a way." Stroking his hand over her hair, he murmured, "I'll go so you can get some sewing done, but please think about this and realize that I wouldn't care if you went barefoot and wore jeans. You would be the only woman there who I would be able to see anyway."

As soon as the door closed behind Rand, Lainie sank onto the couch and burst into tears.

And in his room Joey, who had heard most of the conversation, rolled over and put his face in his pillow. As softly as he could, he prayed. *"God, I don't understand why Lainie should have to hurt so bad. Can't you help her? Can't you get her a dress? Something real pretty? Can't you?"*

The next morning when he woke up, Joey had an idea. He would talk to Rosa. Rosa would know what to do.

Indeed, Rosa did know what to do. She stepped in and took complete charge of the problem, and Lainie never knew what hit her.

The little matter of obtaining the material was

taken care of almost immediately. Efrain had a cousin who had a friend who knew someone who owed him a favor. Through that dubious connection, they were able to obtain the material for the gown at next to nothing, at least according to Rosa. Lainie wasn't allowed to ask the price. It was their gift to her, Rosa had said tearfully. After all, she and Efrain had never had any children of their own, and wasn't Lainie just like their very own daughter? After that declaration Lainie couldn't find it within herself to turn down their loving offer.

The labor for the construction of the dress came even easier. As soon as Rosa explained the matter to the ladies of the garment factory, they all entered into the project with great enthusiasm. Sewing in snatches when they could—mostly on their lunch hours and after work—it took them four days. Cinderella, with her birds and mice, couldn't have had a better crew making her gown, Lainie decided.

Ethel was the cutter. She was a big woman, five feet eleven, who had raised eight children single-handedly. When she had been pregnant with the last of her children, her husband had taken off. She often said her fondest wish was to find him again, show him a picture of the eight kids, and then punch his lights out. Ethel could eat truck fenders for breakfast, Lainie thought.

Then there was Tammy Ahn. She was a bright-eyed Vietnamese woman in her twenties who, with her tiny hands, attended to the fine details such as tucks and hand-stitched hems. When Tammy had first come to America with her family after the fall of Saigon, she had decided she should have an

American name. One day she happened to catch the old Sandra Dee movie *Tammy Tell Me True* on television. Instantly she knew she had found herself a name, but, for a brief while, it had been a toss-up between either Tammy or Sandra Dee. Ethel often said they should all be glad she hadn't been watching *Gidget*.

Genevieve was a middle-aged woman. Gray-haired, half-glasses perched on her nose, soft spoken and invariably kind, she had buried four husbands to date. To amuse themselves the ladies kept up with the health of her fifth husband. She helped Tammy with the rolled-edged hems of the sheer silk panels of the dress. She also did the final fitting on Lainie.

Lola was the garment factory's resident man-chaser. Loudmouthed, but with a heart of gold, she announced to all and sundry that Lainie was going to a ball, not a funeral, and they should lower the neckline and put a split up the side of the sheath. Fortunately saner minds prevailed. Lola fussed that her wisdom and experience were being ignored; but once she saw the gown on Lainie, she pronounced that with a body like Lainie's, a gunnysack would look sexy. To celebrate Lola got herself a hot date and went off to a demolition derby.

And last but not least, there was Walter, the janitor for the garment factory. Nearly bald, with apple-red cheeks, he was in his early sixties and a little slow—Walter and his broom never reached high speeds. He also couldn't sew a stitch, but he had long had a bit of a crush on Lainie, and he really wanted to help. So the ladies took up a collection, gave him a swatch of material, and sent him out to buy shoes to match. But after he had gone, they all had second thoughts. *What*, they asked one another, were they doing sending a man who wore shirts with parrots printed on them, out to buy shoes to match a ball gown?

To the amazement of them all, however, including Walter, he proudly came back with a pair of delicate, strappy, high-heeled sandals that had been dyed to match the exact color of Lainie's dress. Everyone cheered.

The night of the ball, Lainie stood before her mirror staring at herself in disbelief. The dress was made up of two weights of golden-yellow silk. The underdress was a strapless sheath of heavy silk, the bodice a large bow that covered her breasts. The knot in the center of the bow pulled the material down to expose a deep cleavage and reveal the tantalizing swell of her breasts above the glistening fabric. From below her breasts shimmering panels fell in a lighter-weight silk, floating out around her with her slightest movement.

Lainie had brushed her hair to one side and secured it there with the carved ebony comb Rosa had lent her, so that, across one shoulder and down one breast was a straight fall of gleaming black hair.

Dancing around her, Joey chanted, "Lainie is the prettiest girl in the whole wide world! Lainie is the prettiest girl in the whole wide world!"

"Thank you, honey, but I just wish I weren't so nervous."

"Nervous! What do you have to be nervous about?" Rosa scoffed. "Rand Bennett is one lucky *hombre* to have you go with him, and I am going to tell him so too."

That made her even more nervous. "No, Rosa, don't. Please. You either, Joey. I'll be fine, honest."

"Yes, you will," Rosa stated positively. "I don't want you to worry about a thing, and since Joey is sleeping over with me tonight, you can stay out as long as you want."

A knock sounded at the door, and before she could stop him, Joey rushed to answer it. Sometimes, Lainie thought wryly, she had a little too much help. She heard Joey say, "Wait until you see Lainie. She's the prettiest girl in the whole world."

Rand's laughing reply reached through the bedroom door to her. "I haven't even seen her yet, and I absolutely agree with you, Joey."

"Lainie!" Joey called. "Come on out!"

"Great," she muttered under her breath. "I feel like a girl on her first date." She looked at Rosa, whose eyes had filled with tears. She whispered, "Thank you." Then she picked up her purse and went out into the living room.

A moment later she was wishing that she could have a picture of Rand's expression as he turned around and for the first time saw her in her ballgown. But then in the next moment she decided she didn't really need a picture, for she would remember it all her life. His look seemed to combine several emotions—including admiration and desire—and it boosted her confidence considerably.

Unable to take his eyes off her, Rand walked slowly toward her. He wanted so badly to touch her, but Rosa and Joey were watching every move he made, so he reached for her hand and just held it for a minute while he tried to take in how beautiful she looked tonight.

He had told her the truth when he had said it didn't make any difference to him what she wore to the ball. But he had known it would matter to her, very much, so he had offered to buy her a dress. When that didn't work, he had gone to Rosa to see if he could perhaps involve her in a little white lie that would allow Lainie to think Rosa was giving her a dress when in actuality he would be buying it. He had wanted her to come with him so badly, he had been willing to do just about anything. But Rosa had been one step ahead of him, and he couldn't begin to express his gratitude to her.

Aware that Joey and Rosa were waiting for some kind of reaction from him, he leaned down and kissed Lainie very lightly. "Joey's right," he murmured. "You are the most beautiful girl in the world."

Putting one foot behind her leg, she dipped into a little curtsy. "Thank you, sir."

"I really hate to share you with all those people who are going to be there tonight, but I guess we have to go."

"Go, go!" Rosa shooed them out the door, like a mother hen would her chicks. "And remember, stay out as long as you like."

The ballroom of one of Houston's highest-priced hotels had been transformed into an enchanted fairyland forest. Tiny lights embedded in Lucite flashed on and off and were patterned by a computer to appear as if they were flowing around the room. The walls had been covered with a mirror-like silver paper that caught the lights and reflected them back out into the room. Sheer silkscreened panels were suspended from the ceiling. The panels were of trees, some verdantly green, others with flowering vines twining high into their branches, and they were placed throughout the ballroom to make the guests feel as if they were moving in a bewitching, magic forest that glittered. The elite of Houston society added sparkle too with their jewels and laughter.

Lainie soaked it all up, enjoying herself to the hilt. Rand kept her close to his side, proudly introducing her to his friends, whispering little confidences to her concerning this person or that person, and generally making her feel very, very special.

At one point he gave a short speech. Standing on the dais in his formal evening attire, he was very much the distinguished, illustrious surgeon, presenting a knowledgeable, serious face to the group as he eloquently reminded those present of the important cause that they were all there for.

Maybe she was being presumptuous, Lainie thought, but she couldn't help but feel a tingle of pride that perhaps she knew him better than anyone in the room. For she and she alone knew how tender he could look when he tucked a ragged teddy bear into the arms of a sleeping little boy. And she knew how funny he could be when he was playing a joke on her, like the day he had made her climb over his brick wall while he went through the gate.

And then there was his passion—a whole other subject entirely. She knew she had experienced only a portion of it. Did she have the courage to give herself up to it completely?

The trouble was, the more determined she became to maintain her independence, the more he seemed to undermine it. So far neither of them was winning. Or maybe they both were. She no longer knew. The boundary lines she tried to draw never seemed to stay the same.

The speech and dinner over, Rand led her out onto the dance floor. She came into his arms, all softness and grace. Her long skirt rustled against his legs, and he could feel his muscles harden at the contact of her slim, supple body against his.

Gazing down at her, he could see the lovely way her black hair glistened under the lights, and the tantalizing way her breasts rose, firm and round, above the golden yellow silk of her gown. His arms tightened around her and he pulled her even closer into him, so that he could feel as much of her against him as was decently possible in a public place. "I've been waiting all night to get you in my arms," he murmured.

Her jade eyes shone with happiness, and her blood sang with a heated excitement. "I'm having a wonderful time."

"I'm glad. You look like an exotic butterfly in a forest of lights."

Her laughter mingled with the music, stimulating Rand's senses. He bent to nibble on her earlobe and picked up the warmly erotic scent of her skin. It intoxicated him. He wanted to taste all of her, have all of her, and in return, be everything to her.

Within the circle of Rand's arms, Lainie forgot that they weren't alone. They danced, yet barely moved. Rather it was the room that seemed to move around them, the lights and the colors blurring as they whirled dizzyingly around the two of them.

She focused on Rand's eyes, making them her center. In them she saw so much. Much as the silver-covered walls of the room reflected back the lights, the hunger that steadily grew in her was reflected back to her from his eyes, doubling its intensity. His hunger burned into her, creating a craving that consumed and throbbed.

"Come home with me. I want to be alone with you."

She nodded, denial never entering her mind.

The Tudor mansion that was Rand's home had an atmosphere of old-world charm to it, but had state-of-the-art electronics governing it. Made up of dark woods and polished surfaces, rich fabrics and plush carpets, it was a successful blend of three centuries, the best of the old and the new. Burgundy, forest-green, gold, and eggshell swept throughout the house. It was an unexpectedly dignified house, and Lainie decided that it suited Rand perfectly.

He carelessly tossed his jacket and tie in the direction of a velvet-covered monk's bench. Then, watching her carefully, he led her from room to room. The rooms seemed to take on a new life and a new warmth with her in them, he discovered. Having her in his home was just as he had imagined it would be, and, if possible, his feelings strengthened and grew.

At one point she turned to him and said, "You have a beautiful house, Rand. You must be very proud of it."

She meant what she said, he mused. She liked the house, but she wasn't overly impressed by it. He had seen the look of envy and avarice in other people's gazes as they had surveyed it. But in Lainie's clear jade eyes, he could find only her image of him, and it made him feel about ten feet tall.

The final room they entered was the master bedroom. In the middle of the room was a giant carved canopied Chippendale bed. Its hangings and spread were of the identical tapestry print.

She turned, intending to remark on the bed, but the words died in her throat. Rand was standing quite still, but it was apparent that a sensual tension had tightened every muscle in his body. He made no move toward her, yet she couldn't have been more affected if he had pulled her into his arms and kissed her until she was senseless.

Her heart slammed against her ribs. He was already making love to her. She felt no shock, no hesitation. There was very little left to be said between them, she decided on the instant. In this moment of time, no matter the consequences, she needed to belong to him, to let his strength take her over.

The silken panels of her gown fluttered around her as she slowly glided toward him. Drawn by the force of the desire that was pulsating between them, she could do nothing else. Whether they made love or not was no longer a matter of choice. It was inevitable.

Her hands went to the fine white cloth of his shirt and she began to undo the studs one by one. As the shirt gradually parted, Lainie brought her mouth to rest on each section of his newly exposed skin, letting her tongue flick out to lick the male taste of him into her mouth.

A tremor racked through Rand, and his hands slid between her arms and her breasts, so that the palms of his hands were cushioned against the full sides of her breasts and his thumbs rested on the swelling flesh just above the silk.

Her legs weakened, but her resolve to continue her exploration didn't. She reached his waist and pulled the shirt free, then paused, all at once unsure. As she glanced at him, she felt his thumbs slide under the bodice of her dress to flick across the hardened tips of her breasts.

She closed her eyes as a wave of ecstasy crashed through her, and she began to tremble. His hands tightened against her breasts and his thumbs ceased their movements, so that they rested squarely on the rigid tips of her nipples—all the more erotic for what he *wasn't* doing.

"Lainie," he groaned, "I can stop right now, but ten seconds from now I can't promise anything."

The nearly naked need in his voice changed her tentativeness. Her hands reached behind her and slowly drew the zipper of her dress down. The silk garment slipped to the floor in a golden-yellow drift, and she was left wearing nothing but the sandals on her feet and a pair of panties.

There was an audible intake of his breath, and his mouth lowered to the taut peak of one breast and gently suckled, then his hand smoothed down her flat stomach and under her panties. Thrills rippled through her body. "Rand . . . oh, Rand."

"Tell me what you want."

"I want you to make the trembling stop."

"I can do that," he said almost roughly. "But first I'm going to make the trembling worse."

Lainie's body grew liquid, and he picked her up into his arms and carried her to the bed. Her sandals dropped from her feet. In only a moment he had disposed of his clothes and had joined her on the soft, wide bed. She welcomed him by winding her arms around his neck and helping him push her panties down her long legs and then off. Now they were flesh against flesh. His mouth ground into hers, and his tongue thrust urgently.

Digging her heels into the bed so that she could get better leverage, she arched against him. She wanted him so. His hands were exploring her slowly, inch by satin inch, driving her to the brink. "Rand . . ."

"Easy, love," he said hoarsely, realizing that his control was slipping fast. His hand ran over her naked skin, down to the warm depths of her inner thighs. His fingers found her warm and ready for him. Feeling her twist against him, he knew he could take it no more. He entered her, leaving them both gasping. Desperately wanting to please her, he slowed his pace, moving in and out of her with long, powerful strokes. The hard length of him ignited a million pleasure points inside her, gently abrading delicate tissue until her entire body was alive with a fiery joy. And then a tiny cry caught in the back of her throat as her mind closed down, and Rand took her to a place she had never known existed.

Lainie couldn't tell how long it had been that she had rested secure in his arms. She knew only that the night was going too fast. They had made love twice, and she felt tired, but absolutely glowing.

She wished she could think of a way to describe the way Rand made love to her. His lovemaking was complete, assuredly, and it was also thorough. But it was so much more than that, she mused. It was as if every cell of his body and mind became involved.

"Can't you sleep?" he whispered, his lips finding lingering dampness on her temple and kissing it.

"I can't let myself. I need to go home."

"Give me one good reason." His fingers took a handful of her hair and began combing it across him, so that it lay over his chest in a shimmering black fan.

"Joey."

"Rosa is taking care of him. If you're not there when he wakes up, she'll give him breakfast."

"But what is he going to think when he sees me coming home in broad daylight in the same dress that I left home in last night?"

"Let's see." He pretended to ponder her question. "Given that Joey is still very much an innocent little boy, and unaware of the wonderful things that men and women can do to each other, he'll probably just think that the party lasted all night long."

As she turned her head to look at him her hair was dragged an inch or so across him, raising shivers of delight on his skin. "You're very fast."

"Sometimes, not always." A light blush stained her skin, and he looked at her in tender amazement. "I can't believe that after what we've just shared, you can still blush with me."

"You know well and good that I meant you were fast with an answer. Besides, I'm serious. I need to leave."

"In a little while," he agreed.

Lainie knew Rand was trying yet again to get around her, but she didn't care. She made no move to leave, enjoying the warmth and security of his arms, the steady rise and fall of his chest, the idle playing of his fingers in her hair. And in just a few minutes she fell asleep.

Whenever Joey spent the night at Rosa's, he slept on the couch. That night, just before he fell asleep, he remembered he had something to do. Getting down on his knees beside the bed, he got right to it.

"Hi, God. I just wanted to say thanks for the dress. Lainie looked really pretty. You should have seen her! Rand thought she looked pretty too, 'cause he kissed her and everything before they left for the party. Things are going great now. So if you could just have Rand ask Lainie to marry him, it will fix everything, and I won't

bother you anymore." He thought for a minute. *"Well, not as much anyway. Amen."*

Lainie made it home by ten and only just managed to change into her jeans before Rosa came bustling over to tell her that Efrain had taken Joey to church, so that she could hear all about the wonderful ball.

Lainie related the details of the decorations, the music, and the food, using as much vivid description as she could. She even touched lightly on Rand's house, but conveniently didn't mention the hours between midnight and dawn that she had spent in his bed.

Rosa didn't ask for an accounting of the missing hours, as Lainie had been afraid she would. Instead, her eyes bright with happiness, she asked, "So then you and the good doctor are serious?"

"No." Lainie shook her head.

The happiness left Rosa's eyes and her voice climbed incredulously. "It's not serious, and you spent the night with him?"

Lainie jumped up and walked to the sink to get herself a drink of water. "Oh, all right, it's serious!" She stared down into the glass of water a minute before she added, "And I don't know what to do about it."

"What's his problem, *niña*?" It was obviously incomprehensible to Rosa that it could be Lainie's problem.

"It's not him, it's me!" She whirled around. "I think about him too much. I look forward to his phone calls too much. I like being with him too much. I enjoyed the ball too much!"

"And afterward?" the older woman asked shrewdly.

"Too much," Lainie confirmed and sat back down again.

Rosa twisted her mouth and shook her head at the same time, showing that she was truly perplexed. "I do not understand this *too much*. You need the good doctor in your life. Up until now you have spent your days and nights working, studying, and taking care of Joey. It's no good."

"It was what I wanted to do," Lainie retorted defensively.

"So you did it. *Bueno.* You proved to yourself what you can accomplish on your own. But now you need more. You need this man. He is good for you, *querida*. And I would say that you are good for him too."

"I don't think so."

"Bah! You think a smart man like that would be coming around here as often as he does if he did not think you weren't good for him? He knows a good thing when he sees it."

"Rosa, think about it. Rand is a famous doctor. What am I?"

"You are a good, good girl, fine and honest, that's what. If he is as smart as you say—"

"He's brilliant," Lainie said loyally. "Medical students come from all over the world to hear him lecture. And he's charming. He can get around me just about anytime he wants to." She dropped her head into her hands. "Oh, Rosa, what am I going to do? I shouldn't let this go any further. I saw what happened to mother, and because of it I've lived my life with the idea that I would never become too dependent on a man."

"Lainie, you have got to understand. It is not bad to be dependent on Rand. You'd have to be *loca* to think that he is like Spence. And neither are you your mother. You are so much stronger than she ever was." She patted Lainie's hand. "Listen to me, *querida*. I know. Everything will work out for the best. You will see."

Lainie had her doubts about things working out for the best, and her doubts grew stronger when Monday afternoon came and she received a phone call.

Walter came ambling up to her. "Efrain is out on the loading dock, and I was in his office when the phone rang. A man asked to speak to you."

Her brows knitted in concern. No one ever called her at work unless it was an emergency. With one recent emergency so fresh in her mind, she couldn't help jumping to conclusions. "Who is it?"

Walter shook his head. "I don't rightly know and he didn't say. He just asked to speak to you."

"Thank you." Lainie didn't waste time asking any more questions. She hurried to the office. "Hello?"

"You've grown into a beautiful woman, but then I always told your mother that you would."

A cold vice gripped her heart. The voice on the phone belonged to Spence Gordon, Joey's father. She reached for Efrain's chair and sat down at his desk.

When her mother had died and Lainie had taken Joey to live with her, she had hoped that she would never have to see him again. That hope wasn't a naive one either. Basically neglect and lack of interest had always prevailed in Spence's attitude toward his son.

A couple of times Lainie had contacted him to request that he let her become Joey's legal guardian. He had flatly refused. Not because of any love he held for Joey, she was convinced, but because he was a truly unpleasant and obnoxious man. So she had been forced temporarily to shelve the idea of becoming Joey's guardian. She hadn't had the money to fight Spence, and in addition she had been afraid that her lack of money and education would prejudice the courts against her. While they might not think Spence was the ideal father, he was Joey's *real* father.

Besides the two times she had gotten in touch with him, there had been only one other time she had had any contact with him since her mother's death. One night, after Joey had gone to bed, Spence had showed up at her apartment, drunk and menacing. The visit had been out of the blue and therefore that much more threatening. She had had to do some fancy footwork to convince him to leave, but she had managed him then and she would do so now too.

"What do you want, Spence?"

"Just to check up on my boy, what else?" He sounded lighthearted and of good cheer, Lainie thought sourly. Unless she missed her guess, the good cheer had come from a bottle.

"Why now? We haven't heard from you in close to two years."

"I've been . . . busy. And by the way I see you've been busy too."

"I have no idea what you're talking about."

"Why your picture, sweetheart! Haven't you seen your picture? It's in both papers."

"Don't call me sweetheart."

"Yes, sir. When I saw you at that fancy society gig on the arm of that Dr. Bennett, I said to myself, 'Lainie's coming up in the world.' "

"Was there something else you wanted, Spence?"

His tone lost a lot of its joviality. "Yeah, as a matter of fact there was. I'll be dropping by in a day or two to see you—oh, and Joey, too, of course."

"Don't you dare! Do you hear me, Spence? Joey's happy. Your visit will only leave him confused. He doesn't even remember you."

"Well, then just maybe I ought to see the boy more often. That way he wouldn't get so confused."

Lainie tried to remain calm, but she had no comeback.

"Think about it, sweetheart. A boy ought to have a daddy. Good-bye for now."

When Efrain found her fifteen minutes later, Lainie was still sitting at his desk, and her face was very pale under the harsh fluorescent lighting.

"What is it?"

"It's Spence."

Efrain let loose with a whole stream of Spanish that was so profane, Lainie decided not to listen. It took a while, but he finally wound down. When he finished, he huffed, "I thought we were rid of that bastard."

"So did I. Efrain, I don't know what I'm going to

do. He talked about seeing more of Joey. I can't let that happen."

Efrain placed his hand on her shoulder, wanting to comfort. "No, no. Of course, you can't. But I don't understand. Why should he suddenly want to see Joey after all this time? He abandoned his son and now he wants to see him. I don't like this. It's no good, no good."

"I agree, and it doesn't make any sense either. That's what frightens me. I've always been able to figure him out."

"You know, he could just be bluffing. Maybe he was in a mean mood and wanted to give you a bad time. He doesn't want Joey any more than you want to let your little brother go."

Her jade eyes stared sightlessly. "I hope you're right, Efrain. I hope you're right."

Six

As the days passed and Spence didn't try to contact her, Lainie's mind eased. She fervently hoped that he had left town, and that the phone call had been just one of his periodic harassment tactics. She was convinced that he rarely even thought about her and Joey. Yet she knew him to be a highly erratic person, and consequently the fear that sooner or later he would contact her remained.

In the meantime Rand was becoming more and more integrated into her life. While respecting and understanding that she needed a certain number of hours a week for the extra sewing she did, he also managed to carve out a number of hours that they could spend together. How he had gone about fitting himself so neatly into her life, she hadn't quite figured out yet. All she knew was that she had never been happier.

Rand sometimes came by, picked up Joey, and the two of them would go off for a few hours by themselves. They seemed genuinely to enjoy being with each other, and of course, Rosa adored the 'good doctor Rand' as she called him.

Today, however, there was just Rand and herself. It was Sunday, and he had suggested that they spend the afternoon at his house. She had readily agreed. She was more than used to his touch now. It seemed she constantly hungered for it.

Sitting close to him as he drove toward his house, she idly commented, "It looks like it might rain any minute."

He glanced at the sky. All morning, clouds had been forming, breaking up, and forming again. "I don't think so. Those clouds don't look too dedicated to me. At any rate the rain will hold off until we get to the house." He glanced at her. "If it wasn't so warm, it would be a perfect afternoon to spend in front of the fire. As it is I guess we'll have to be content with looking at my etchings."

"Etchings? The doctor has etchings!" She shook her head. "I'm disappointed. I was sure you could be more original than that, Rand."

"Okay, how about this? You should wear skirts more often. You have beautiful legs."

Somewhat self-consciously, she ran her hands across the cotton print skirt she had put on that morning on an impulse. "I think I can remember wearing this skirt in high school, but it hasn't aged too badly, and I decided I needed a change from my jeans."

Looking over at her, he took her hand. With the skirt she was wearing the cowl-neck knit top that she had worn on their first picnic. The forest-green color deepened the jade of her eyes, and her hair flowed straight and shining down her back. He wondered if she would believe him if he told her just exactly how beautiful she was to him, no matter what she wore. He decided she wouldn't. But someday, he vowed, someday, she would believe him. And this afternoon, if all went as he hoped, she would begin to understand just how much she really did mean to him.

Reaching the street on which his estate was located, he turned the corner. But they had gone only a little way when his car began to wheeze and sputter.

"What's wrong, Rand?"

"I don't know." His eyes scanned the gauges and dials that would have done any jet cockpit proud. "I'm afraid I don't know much about cars."

"I can't believe it!" She clapped her hands together in glee. "That's two things."

"Two things?"

"Two things you don't know anything about— cars and weather."

"I know about weather," he explained patiently. "But as for cars, I figure if I pay an exorbitant sum of money for the thing, see to it that it has gas on a more or less regular basis, then when I put my key in the ignition and turn it, it should run. It's only fair. I can't be bothered with a car that won't hold up its end of the deal."

Lainie leaned over and quickly scanned the instruments. "I don't quite know how to tell you this, Doctor, but in this instance, I think it's you that's fallen down on your end of the deal."

"What are you talking about?"

"Gas. You're running on empty."

Coasting the car to a stop by the curb, Rand studied the gas gauge thoughtfully. "I wonder if anyone's thought of inventing a car that would drive itself to the gas station and fill itself up?"

She could hardly contain her laughter. "You know what I think?"

"What?"

"I think running out of gas is one of the oldest ploys in the book."

"You do, huh?"

"Yep." She allowed herself a slight smile. "It ranks right up there with 'Let me show you my etchings.' "

"I really do have etchings, you know."

"If I have to walk to get to them," she warned, "they had better be good!"

"We're not as far from the house as you think." He pointed toward the tall brick wall that ran parallel to the street. "The garden where we had our first picnic is right behind that wall."

Lainie looked in dismay at the wall in question. "I'm *not* climbing that thing again."

"You won't have to. The gate is not that far away."

"But won't it be locked?"

"As it happens I have the key. I'm on the most intimate of terms with the owner."

"Oh, yes, I remember that now. Okay, then, let's get going before it starts raining."

"We won't get wet, Lainie. I'm telling you, it's not going to rain for a long while yet."

They reached the gate and Rand unlocked it.

"See, this key fits the gate, plus an assortment of other doors around the place. I keep my everyday life very simple, because there are too many other more important and intricate matters that my mind needs to focus on."

Lainie understood perfectly what he meant. Quite literally, lives depended on him, this man who walked so easily beside her, holding her hand. And she knew all too well the greatly significant work he did. She admired him for it, but she had never dwelled on it. She could only be aware of him as a man who was able to make her laugh with happiness or cry with passion.

And she couldn't resist teasing him. "I assume filling the car with gas is *not* one of those things your mind focuses on."

"Someone usually does that for me," he admitted. "It's imperative that I reach the hospital in the minimum amount of time and with zero difficulty."

They had walked only a short distance into the garden when he stopped and pulled her into his arms. "I need to modify what I said. I keep my everyday life simple with one very important exception."

The air around them was warm and fragrant and heavy with moisture. She leaned against his chest and looked up at him. "What's that, Doctor?"

"You," he returned seriously. "Since I've met you, I find myself waiting to see you. No matter what has happened during the day, when I finally am able to be with you, you make all my cares and worries vanish. And on those days that I can't see you, I'm miserable until I can. You, Lainie, are very important to my days and to my nights."

Sometimes it just wasn't fair the way he could get to her, she reflected. Then his mouth came down on hers.

His mouth could tease, it could torment, it could incite, Lainie mused. This time it did all three. Nibbling tiny kisses across her face to her ears and down her neck, he found the most unlikely spots to touch lightly and make spring to life until she was tingling all over with a sensual pleasure. He tasted her, he savored her, taking his time, and she wondered briefly how he could remain standing when she felt so weak. Pressing against him, her fingers threaded into his hair. When his lips finally reached hers, she was almost crazy, ready for the gently grating feel of his tongue, ready for the peculiar satisfaction she received when his tongue thrust in and out of her mouth.

There was something primal and exciting about being in Rand's arms in the middle of this beautiful garden. Completely alone, their privacy was protected by high walls, a low, opaque sky, and thousands and thousands of colorful, fragrant blossoms. He lowered them to a place on the grass that was particularly thick and cushiony, lying her down so that her black hair spread around her head. "I love you, Lainie," he whispered, "and I want to make love to you now."

"Yes, Rand . . . oh, yes."

Piece by piece their clothes were discarded. Inch by inch each explored the other's body. And when the rain came, it was soft and warm, cooling their fevered skin. They noticed only that it heightened the sensuality of their lovemaking, and that, with it, the skin of the other became smoother, slicker, making it easier to glide their hands, their legs, and their tongues over.

Fire in the rain. It came down around them, misting them both with equal intensity. She submitted. He dominated. She dominated. He submitted. Their skin began to glisten with beads of rain. Steam rose around them.

The air grew hazy with desire. Rand moved over her and into her. He groaned his pleasure, feeling her contract around him. She gasped, feeling his hard length fill her. As he thrust and she arched, their bodies met and joined. Then as he withdrew and she pulled her hips away, they briefly parted. But always they would meet again. There was too much ecstasy to be had not to, too much of a building promise of more.

The rain increased as did their rhythm. Lying on a carpet of green in the middle of an enchanted flowerland, they reached together and found what, at the moment of fulfillment, they both became absolutely certain that no one else could ever give them.

Minutes later, with a soft spring rain falling on them, they lay in each other's arms, laughing.

"You're wet," Rand whispered.

"And you're very observant." She kissed the tip of his nose. "And very wet." She kissed the edge of his chin. "And also very good."

"That's kind of you to say." He pressed his mouth to the center of her forehead.

"Not at all." She touched his temple with her

tongue and came away with rainwater. "Actually you're too good."

"There's no such thing as too good," he said very definitely, and drew his tongue over her lips.

"For the peace of my mind and my body there is." Her fingers plowed shallow rows of indentations into the muscled skin of his back.

"Ah, your body. Now. There you have struck on a subject I happen to be an expert on."

She drew away. "Oh?"

"He pulled her back. "But not as expert as I plan to become."

Turning her head toward the sky, she let the rain shower over her face. "Let me ask you something."

"Sure." He lifted his head until his face was over hers and he was shielding her from the rain.

"What would you say if I suggested that we go into the house?"

He dropped a kiss to her lips. "I'd say that I'm surprised I didn't think of it."

Lainie sat on the end of Rand's bed, wrapped in his terry robe. They had taken a shower and had made love again. In the wet, steamy heat of his shower Lainie had discovered that there didn't seem to be any limit to the pleasure they could bring each other.

Now Rand was behind her, hairbrush in one hand, hair dryer in the other, blowing her hair dry. The warm heat against her scalp and the long, gentle strokes of the brush made her feel quite cosseted and utterly relaxed. Yet something kept niggling at the back of her mind.

"I think we should make love again," Rand shouted over the whir of the hair dryer.

"What?"

He clicked the dryer off. "I said, I think we should make love again."

She fell backward against him and tilted her face so that she could see his eyes. "Okay, but any particular reason why?"

He twisted her around so that she was lying in his arms. "To see if we can make love when we're dry."

He wore only a towel around his waist, and she snuggled her face against his warm, bare chest. "You don't actually have any doubts, do you?"

"Not really. I just thought it sounded like a good excuse."

Her arm began creeping around his neck, but then stopped. She had just remembered what it was that was nagging at her, and a strange hurting pressure settled in her chest. She pushed against him so that she could sit up and see him better. "Rand, in the garden . . . you said that you loved me!"

The smile on his face died. "I do, Lainie. I hadn't meant to blurt it out like that during lovemaking. I wanted to tell you under more calm and controlled circumstances. But as usual, where you're concerned, I rushed my fences." Her jade eyes had widened, and in their depths, he could see clouds of turmoil. "I hope you believe me, Lainie, because I do love you."

"I don't know." Dragging her fingers through her hair, she discovered that it was completely dry, and she remembered the care Rand had taken to get it that way.

"Lainie." His finger came out to turn her face to him. "There's something else. And again, I had planned to wait until the special dinner I was going to prepare for us tonight."

"What is it?" Her mind didn't seem capable of taking her past the fact that he had said he loved her.

Rand let out a long, slow breath. "I want more than anything in the world for you to marry me. Will you?"

Her mouth dropped open, the pressure in her chest increased, and her heart began to beat wildly. "You can't be serious!"

"I've never been more serious in my life. Please say you'll marry me."

She clambered off the bed and began to pace. "It makes no sense! I'm not cut out to be the wife of a doctor."

With every step she took, his stomach tied itself into one more painful knot. He had expected her to be surprised. He had even expected some resistance. But at no time had he considered that she might react this vehemently. Forcing himself to remain cool, he lounged back against the pillows and crossed his legs. "I wasn't aware there was a cookie cutter for a doctor's wife."

"You must know what I mean. You need a well-dressed Junior League type, Rand. Someone who would be right at home serving on this or that committee, someone who would look good in gold jewelry and driving a Mercedes."

He exploded. "For God's sake, what does gold

jewelry or a Mercedes or even the Junior League have to do with anything? This is between you and me, Lainie. Nothing else enters into the picture."

She stopped and looked at him. "Okay. You and me, then. We're too different."

"I know what I need, Lainie, and I also know that you and I being different is one of the lamest arguments you could give me. Our lovemaking alone could disprove that one."

"Just because we make love together well, doesn't mean—"

"There's more and you know it." He patted the bed beside him. "Stop pacing and come here. Sit down and let's talk this out."

Dammit! What was wrong with her? she wondered. Why hadn't she seen this coming? She supposed that she had been living in a dreamworld, enjoying all the time they spent together, never taking her thinking one step further to consider that he might want to marry her. But he did. He wasn't misleading her or playing a game with her. He was being completely honest with her. He had even admitted that he knew he was rushing her.

So what was her problem? she asked herself. But she knew the answer. Over the years she had grown to distrust what loving a man could do to a woman. She had worked very hard to be independent. Then Rand had come into her life. She hadn't readjusted her thinking exactly, she had just slowly relaxed and for the first time in her life had begun to see what a real relationship with a man could be like. But now he was asking for more than she could give. How could she make him understand?

She climbed up on the bed and into his arms, so that she lay beside him with her cheek resting on his bare shoulder. "I don't think I can ever marry anyone, Rand."

"Do you love me?"

The question sent a shock wave tearing through her. Since she had met him, she had been so busy making sure that he didn't run over her with his strong personality that she hadn't even considered whether she loved him or not. But as soon as he had posed the question, she had known. She did love him. Damn! Damn! Damn! It had been such a gradual, easy process that she hadn't realized what was happening to her.

"Do you love me?" he repeated quietly.

She couldn't be anything but honest with him. "Yes, but I can't marry you."

Her reply was such that he couldn't even take a minute to exult over the fact that she loved him. He twisted on the bed so that he could see her face better. "Now *you're* talking about something that makes no sense!"

"I'm sorry, Rand, but I could never allow a man to run my life."

"Who's asking you to? Hasn't our time together taught you anything?" She didn't answer, and a long sigh escaped his lips. "No, I guess it hasn't. I've gone too fast."

"Stop it, Rand. I won't let you continue to take all the blame. Granted you do tend to come on too strong at times, but mostly you're wonderful. Besides, you haven't heard me complaining lately, have you?"

"But?"

"But marriage." She shook her head. "It hasn't been in my vocabulary for so long, I can't even think about it rationally. It scares me."

He reached for a strand of her hair. "Then maybe with time . . ."

"I can't promise you anything, Rand."

He stared at her in silence. "All right. But just tell me that you're not going to ask me to stop seeing you, because I couldn't do that."

"I couldn't ask you to," she replied softly, and buried her face against his chest.

On the surface nothing changed. Rand still came over and took her out, sometimes including Joey. But it wasn't the same. Something carefree had gone out of their relationship. They were more careful with each other—more awkward. The newly admitted love ran like an undercurrent through their relationship and made everything more complicated.

It wasn't just her imagination either. Joey had also picked up the vibrations and watched them constantly whenever they were all together. The day Joey asked her if Rand had proposed, she nearly dropped the plate she was holding. She had to tell him yes, and then try to explain why she had turned the proposal down, but she could tell that he hadn't understood.

Then one night after Joey had gone to bed, her worst fears came true. She was sitting up late, sewing, when she heard a light knock on the door. It flashed through her mind that it might be Rand, but on the way to the door, she revised that opinion. He never came over anymore without calling first. Deciding that it must be Rosa, she opened the door, smiling. The smile died on her face.

"Hello, sweetheart. Long time no see."

"Spence." She acted on her first impulse and tried to slam the door.

Neatly blocking it with his foot, he put his hand against the door and shoved. Because she couldn't risk making a scene with Joey asleep in the next room, she was forced to stand aside and let him walk in. As quietly as she could she asked, "What do you want?"

Her open animosity didn't faze him. "Now, is that any way to greet your stepdaddy?"

Lainie eyed him carefully. He didn't appear to have been drinking tonight, she told herself. That was good. It would make it easier to handle him. She wondered briefly if he had stopped drinking, then decided that, by the looks of him, he probably hadn't. Age hadn't made all the changes she could see in him.

When he had married her mother, he had been a nice-looking man. Now his blue eyes weren't as clear as they had been at one time, and his blond hair, once the color of Joey's, had darkened. There was a certain puffiness under his eyes, the slightest beginning of jowls under his chin, and more than a suggestion of a paunch at his stomach. Lainie wished her mother could see him.

"Spence, unless you've come to give me legal guardianship of Joey, I want you to leave."

"Funny you should bring that up, sweetheart, because that's just what I've come to talk to you about."

Her heart leapt at the idea of finally becoming Joey's legal guardian, but she forced herself to remain calm. Even if Spence were serious about it, she knew he wouldn't just hand over the guardianship without trying to get something in return.

He plopped himself down in the middle of her sofa. "Got any beer?"

"No," she said through gritted teeth. "And please don't talk so loud. Joey's sleeping."

He looked toward the bedroom door with an interest that was clearly exaggerated. "Is that a fact? How is he anyway?"

He was stalling for time, and she knew it. "What did you mean when you said that you came to talk about Joey's guardianship? Are you finally willing to let me have it? It is in Joey's best interests, you know."

"Well, now, not so fast. Let's talk about you first." His eyes slowly investigated her in such a way that, by the time he was through, she felt as if she should take a bath. "You're lookin' mighty fine, mighty fine." He paused before delivering the punch line. "I bet that doctor of yours thinks so too."

In her mind she always likened Spence to oil that had oozed into fresh water. He spoiled things for everyone he came into contact with, and this would be no exception. She knew he wasn't through. She remained silent and waited for it to come.

His eyes sharpened. "You're still seeing him, aren't you?"

"That's none of your business!"

He smiled at her angry retort, well satisfied. "Yes

sir, I was awfully glad to see your picture in the paper the other day. That's why I called. You, little girl, have got it made." He cast a contemptuous look around the room. "I don't know what you're still doing in this dump. If you were playing your cards right, you'd be queen of the manor by now over in River Oaks."

The muscles in her stomach tightened. Spence knew that Rand lived in River Oaks, and that could mean he had been checking up on him. She tried to head Spence off the track. "This place is all Joey and I need. He's a very well adjusted little boy, and he loves it here."

He completely ignored the mention of his son. "You know, sweetheart—"

She couldn't help but snap, "Don't call me *sweetheart.*"

He eyed her levelly. "I've always thought you were smart. After all, you knew the exact time to bail out on your mama, now, didn't you? When I came along, you saw the writing on the wall. You knew the money would run out, and you split."

It took everything she had just to stay where she was. She felt like flying at him, with teeth and nails flashing. She gripped her hands together so tightly, she could feel the muscles in her arms tremble. "I'm going to ask you one more time, Spence. Leave."

"Sure. Sure thing, sweetheart. But first I have a little proposition for you. One I think you're going to like."

She knew what he was going to say even before he said it. But because Joey's future was at stake, she had to listen in case she was wrong. She prayed she was wrong, but she wasn't.

"Now, here's the deal. Fifty thousand dollars and I'll sign whatever papers you want giving you guardianship of Joey."

"Fifty thousand dollars! Spence, you've got to be crazy. I can't get that kind of money."

"Sure, you can." He sneered. "That doctor of yours is filthy rich and in a position to be very generous to his pretty girlfriend, namely you. All you have to do is be nice to him, encourage him, and"—he leaned forward for emphasis—"give him what he wants."

"I can't do that Spence. I won't."

"Get the money and Joey is yours. Without it I can't promise anything." He threw a casual glance toward the bedroom door. "Who knows? I just might decide to get fatherly."

Seven

Lainie didn't sleep that night. She just sat and stared at nothing in particular. Her mind reeled with the decisions she was going to be forced to make in the next few hours.

The idea to take Joey and run as far away from Houston and Spence as she could was the first and most instinctive idea that sprang into her mind. After wrestling with it a while, though, she discarded it. If she were alone, it would be different. But she couldn't drag Joey away from all that was familiar to him, and take him into a situation where they would have no friends, no place to stay, and very little money. Then there would be the problem of finding a new job. No, she couldn't do that to him.

But she couldn't let Spence have him either. She knew Spence. He didn't want Joey, yet he was perfectly capable of taking him if she didn't come up with the money, and then what kind of life would Joey have? She shuddered just thinking about it.

She couldn't go to Rosa and Efrain for help. She knew they had a small nest egg, but it was simply that—small and theirs—and she wouldn't ask them for it. They had never had much in the way of material possessions, but they had always been the first there for her, offering help of any kind. No, she wouldn't bring this trouble to them.

That left Rand. He loved her. If she told him she needed fifty thousand dollars, she had no doubt that he would give it to her. But once Spence saw that Rand was willing to give her money, he wouldn't be satisfied with only fifty thousand dollars. He would want more and more. Rand might not mind draining his personal fortune for her and Joey's sake, but she wouldn't be able to bear it.

And that wasn't the only problem. Rand was a great man. If it became public knowledge that he had been paying blackmail money to a man like Spence, it couldn't help but tarnish him and the work he did. She knew Rand wouldn't care about himself and his personal reputation, but if it touched or harmed the work he did, it would wound him irreparably.

Lainie would not do that to Rand. She would never let him be used or hurt because of her.

For so long she had distrusted what loving a man could do to her. She had been able to see only the negative side of it. But now Spence's demands had had an unforeseen result. For the first time she was able to see that loving Rand had made her a better person. Her love for him had strengthened her determination to stand up for herself and for those she loved and to solve her own problems.

It was exceedingly ironic that, at this time, when all her fears about love and marriage had finally been laid to rest, it had become very clear to Lainie that she should break off her relationship with Rand. That would protect Rand, and it would also protect Joey. That *she* would be left unprotected and hurting, she valiantly tried to dismiss from her mind.

Spence had never before asked her for money; he knew she didn't have any. The only reason he had done so this time was because he had seen her relationship with Rand as an untapped gold mine. Once Rand was removed from the picture, she was convinced Spence would crawl back into whatever slime pit he had come from and leave her and Joey alone.

Painful though it was, she finally resolved the matter in her mind sometime before dawn and managed to catch a couple of hours sleep before going into the garment factory. The hours at work passed in a daze. Whether she sewed, whether she spoke with any of her co-workers, or even whether she ate lunch, she wasn't able to say. She only knew that she put in her allotted time and then went home.

That Efrain had called Rosa concerning her was only too evident when Rosa met her at the door.

"*Por dios!* Why didn't you tell me you were sick?"

"I'm not sick, Rosa. I'm just tired."

"You look sick," Rosa stated firmly. "So you are sick."

Lainie pinched the bridge of her nose between

her thumb and forefinger. "Uh, Rosa? I need to see Rand tonight. Do you think you could keep Joey for me?"

The older woman's expression lightened. "Ah! That is *bueno*! You are seeing the good doctor Rand. He will make you feel much better." She waved her hand in the air. "Joey is no problem, no problem."

No, Lainie agreed silently. Joey was not the problem. Rand was, and she had no idea how she was ever going to get through the evening ahead.

Rand studied Lainie from beneath half-lowered lids. Something was wrong. Very wrong, he told himself. He had the same painful knots in his stomach that he had gotten on the night she told him she couldn't marry him.

They were sitting at the kitchen table, and she had just poured them both a tall glass of iced tea. But instead of drinking it, she was absently drawing figures in the condensation on the side of the glass.

He tried to be patient, as he had been trying to be these last couple of weeks. But it was so damn hard to keep from bundling her into his car and taking her to the nearest judge he could find who would marry them.

He had discovered it was a helpless feeling, loving someone this much, yet having to wait until he could make her truly his. He didn't like the feeling one damn bit, but he was determined that she would be his soon. He refused even to consider that Lainie might slip away from him.

"Is there something I can help you with?" he asked quietly.

She jumped at the sound of his voice. "What?"

"You look like you're carrying the weight of the world on your shoulders."

She gave a little laugh, but even to her ears it sounded false. "Nothing like that. But actually there is something I need to tell you."

"I'm listening."

She forced herself to meet his eyes. She would not be a coward about this, she told herself. She wouldn't allow herself to do this halfway. She must make him believe her! Reminding herself that this was for his own good as well as hers and Joey's, she moistened her lips and began. "Rand, I've decided that it would be best for all concerned if you and I didn't see each other again."

Rand felt as if he had been kicked in the gut. Her telling him that they shouldn't see each other again had been a fear of his since the start and now it had actually happened. "Best for *whose* concern?" he asked politely.

God! She had put that wounded look in his eyes! She experienced such a wave of raw pain, she had to drop her eyes in case he saw it. "Yours," she muttered. "Mine. Everyone's."

His fist came down on the table with a thud. "Dammit, Lainie! I won't let you do this to us! What we have is special."

His beautiful hands, she thought miserably. She had reduced them to fists of anger. Trying to ease the tightness that threatened to close her throat, she took a sip of tea. "I'm sorry, Rand. I truly am.

But there's just no way it can work between you and me. You must see that."

"I can't see anything but you, and I haven't been able to for weeks now. I see you in the operating room. I see you in my offices. I see you in my bed."

"There's so much you don't understand, Rand. Things I'll never be able to explain sufficiently to you. I—I suppose I've been on my own too long."

"Oh, hell, yes! Even as we speak, you're pushing all of twenty-six."

She shook her hair away from her face. *When he leaves*, she mused dully, *I'm going to start crying and I may never stop.* "Rand, I saw my mother try to live her life through the men that she loved. I saw what it did to her. And because I did, I'll never be able to give a man a hundred percent of myself."

"You're not your mother," he said, unknowingly repeating Rosa's words.

"I knew you wouldn't understand."

"Okay, you're right. I don't. But it doesn't matter. I'm willing to take whatever percent of you you'll give me."

"You deserve so much more."

"I want you, Lainie."

She looked away. She had known it was going to be hard. She just hadn't realized how hard. And she was doing a terrible job of it. So far all she had succeeded in doing was to tear them both apart. What could she say to him, she wondered helplessly, that would convince him?

He reached his hand across the table to her. "Lainie, listen to me. I love you. Granted I want to marry you, but I accepted it when you said no. I haven't pushed you lately, have I? I've tried to abide by your rules. I've tried to make you happy."

That was it, she realized suddenly. He had just given her the one reason that might convince him that they shouldn't see each other again. Her eyes went back to him. To use this against him would not only be unfair, it would be dishonest. Did she have the courage? she wondered, then decided that it didn't matter whether or not she did. She had to tell him. She couldn't take much more, and she didn't think he could either. They were both bleeding inside.

Still, she could barely force the words out. "I'm not happy."

"What?"

"You haven't made me happy, Rand. Do us both a favor and accept that what we had is over."

Bewilderment contorted his face. "But you said you loved me!"

"I may love you in my fashion, but the fact remains that, basically, I'm miserable."

The confusion in his face, the pain in his voice, was something she knew she would bear the rest of her life.

Where was the laughter now? she questioned herself silently. The sense of fun, the sense of humor, the sense of love—all the things that he had given her over the past weeks. They were gone. In him and in her.

"Good-bye, Rand." She got up. There was no more to be said.

He stood up too. "Good-bye, Lainie," he murmured, and his tone clearly told that he couldn't believe he was saying the words. Tragically she understood his feelings all too well.

Hi, God. It's me, Joey, and I need to talk to you again. Something's happened and I don't understand it. It was all working out so well with Rand and Lainie. He even asked her to marry him, but she said no! I miss Rand a lot. I love him, and I want Lainie to love him too. Can't you make her love him, God? Can't you bring him back?" He opened his eyes and began to get up from his knees, but halfway up he stopped. Kneeling again, he quickly closed his eyes. *"Sorry. I nearly forgot. Amen."*

Rand felt as if someone had performed open-heart surgery on him without the benefit of anesthesia. Any spare minute he had during the following days, he would mentally take out Lainie's words and review them. In his head he ran them backward and forward, he added them and he subtracted them, he took them apart and he put them back together again. And *still* they made no sense to him.

One night around midnight he slammed a glass of Scotch onto a mantel. This hurting was going to stop right now!

Granted, Lainie had some things to work through regarding her views on marriage, but he wouldn't believe that was the problem. He was willing to bet everything he owned that she hadn't meant a word she had said to him, and that it had hurt her to say it just as much as it had hurt him to hear it.

The reason she had said those things didn't bother him so much at the moment. He was confident that sooner or later he would discover the reason. What did bother him was how he was going to get her to change her mind. Moreover, if she refused to continue seeing him, how was he even going to have a chance?

Absently he picked up the glass, tilted it, and let a measure of Scotch slide down his throat. He had never run into a problem like this before. It wasn't like attacking an enemy camp in Montaraz or repairing the defective heart of a patient. Nevertheless, he didn't doubt that he would solve this problem.

Lainie was having an even more difficult time getting through the days without Rand. It was worse than she could ever have imagined. And beside her own personal heartache, she had to contend with Rosa and Joey.

Upon hearing the news, Rosa had declared her *loca*, washed her hands of her, then pulled her to her bosom and told her she should eat something—all in the space of two minutes.

When Joey heard that Rand wouldn't be coming around anymore, he had gotten very quiet and had barely said much of anything since.

And then there was Spence. Once she told him that there was no possibility she could come up with the money, she had thought that he would leave without a word. She had been wrong.

At first he hadn't believed her, but as the days had passed, and he hadn't seen any sign of her going out with Rand, he had grudgingly come to believe that she was telling the truth. But to Lainie's consternation he still contacted her just about every day. He couldn't seem to shake the idea that she could still help him in some way. The question was, What should she do now?

"Rand!" Joey exclaimed happily.

"Hiya, buddy!" He swung the little boy up into his arms. "I've missed you!"

"Have you really?" Joey squealed happily and wound his chubby arms around Rand's neck in a fierce hug. "Lainie said you wouldn't be back, but I just knew she was wrong."

Glancing over the little boy's shoulder, Rand saw Lainie standing in the bedroom door. She had obviously just stepped out of the shower because she was wearing a short white cotton robe that left her arms and legs bare, and her skin had a damp sheen to it. Her hair was wrapped turban-style in a towel.

It had been over two weeks since he had last seen her, held her. And despite the careful plans he had made, if it hadn't been for Joey, he would probably have dragged her into his arms. As it was, he was very grateful for Joey.

He set him down and nodded to her. "Lainie."

"What are you doing here, Rand? And why," she added as an afterthought, "didn't you call?"

"Being patient and following your rules got me

nowhere. I decided to revert to my steamroller tactics."

Lainie pulled the edges of her robe together as best she could. She could feel the thin, slightly wet material clinging to her skin, but there was nothing she could do about it. When she had heard the knock at the door, she had been so afraid it might be Spence, she hadn't even taken the time to dry properly. Now she almost wished that it had been. She could handle her feelings about Spence. She couldn't, however, begin to handle her feelings regarding Rand.

"Joey," she said. "Run next door and stay with Rosa for a little while."

"Aw, Lainie!"

Rand arched one eyebrow at the boy. "Do as your sister says."

"All right, but will you still be here when I get back?"

Rand cast a quick glance at Lainie, then turned back to Joey. "I'm not sure. But if I'm not, I *will* see you again soon. Okay?"

"Okay!" Joey smiled happily and skipped out the door.

Lainie only just resisted the urge to gnash her teeth together. Joey should mind her, not Rand! And why was Rand here anyway?

He saw the anger flare in her eyes. Slowly he walked toward her until he was standing close enough to reach out to her—which is exactly what he did. His long fingers stroked down the sensitive length of her neck. "I've missed you."

She shied away from his touch, much as she had

done the first night she had met him. "Don't do that!"

He smiled because, no matter how she might protest, he had felt the shudder that had raced through her. He folded his arms across his chest. "How have you been?"

"Fine. Never better." Unconsciously she copied him, folding her arms across her chest too. But not before he noticed the pointed tips of her breasts jutting against the cotton robe. "Then you haven't missed me?"

"Not at all," she replied, lying bravely.

"That's good." He nodded, as if considering a diagnosis. "And the reason you pulled away was not because you were affected, but because you are completely over me, right?" Casually, his hand went to the towel wrapped around her hair, and he tugged it off. Her hair came tumbling down in a shining black cascade.

She eyed him warily. "You shouldn't have come, Rand."

"Why?"

His fingers had been combing through her hair for a full minute before she thought to push his hand away. She felt like screaming because of the ease with which her body was giving her away. "Because, if you'll remember, I told you that we shouldn't see each other again."

"Oh, I remember very well. Each word is crystal-clear in my mind. But there are a lot of other memories there too." He looked down at the deep cleavage of her breasts showing above the low **V** neckline of the wrap. "Like the way your body looks without any clothes. Like the way you would look if I took that robe off you."

The raw huskiness of his voice nearly undid her. She dropped her head and her hair fell in a black curtain on either side of her face. "Oh, Rand." Her despair came through even though she had intended otherwise. "Why did you have to come?"

He stepped closer, lifted her face, and then his mouth came down on hers. The kiss was deep and intimate and probing. It demanded response, and just for a little while, she gave it to him. She couldn't help it. A wildfire was racing through her veins, and she was very conscious that they were all alone. They could make love, just one more time, and no one would ever know, Lainie told herself.

He parted her robe so that his hands could cup her breasts and his fingers could caress. She moaned and arched. Then she heard his low husky laugh, and she knew he wanted more than merely to make love with her. With his lips and with his touch he was trying to draw out every one of her secrets. She pushed against him with all her might, and he reluctantly released her.

"That's why I had to come see you," he whispered. "It's been too damn long."

Too long! She could tell him exactly—to the minute—just how long it had been. But she couldn't let the time they had been apart or his kiss matter. She had nearly slipped up. She couldn't do it again. With trembling legs she walked across the room until she was at the front window. The thing to do, she told herself, was to remember just how important it was that she have nothing to do with

Rand. Spence must never be given the means to harm either Joey or Rand.

Only when her breathing had leveled, and her legs had steadied did she spin around. "Please leave."

"Then you haven't changed your mind?"

She arched her eyebrow, attempting a perfect imitation of Rand at his most arrogant. "Of course not. I don't understand why you would think I had. I meant every word I said. Now please, will you leave?" She wouldn't have believed it possible, but attempting to get him out of her life for the second time hurt even worse than the first.

What had he expected? he asked himself angrily. That she would fall into his arms after only one kiss? That whatever it was that was broken between them would be fixed? He cursed silently and shoved his hands into his pockets. "All right. I'll leave, but only after I do what I came to do."

She took a cautious step backward, forgetting that she was already nearly at the wall. "What's that?"

"I came to offer you a job."

"A what?" She would have fallen if the wall hadn't been behind her.

"A job," he repeated, and as if he hadn't just proposed the most preposterous thing in the world, he sat down.

"Doing *what*, for heaven's sake?"

He crossed an ankle over one knee and idly studied the shine on one of his brown loafers. "I think I told you about the clinic that I set up for the underpriviledged, where the patients are predominantly Mexican immigrants, legal and otherwise."

She nodded, reluctant to show interest, but nevertheless both intrigued and puzzled.

"There's a great need for people with bilingual talents, especially in this part of the country. Surely you know that?"

"Of course. Why do you think I want to teach Spanish?"

"Have you thought that you could be using your talents right now? While you're getting your degree?"

"No." She was very definite. "I'm nowhere near the point of finishing the requirements for my degree, plus, because of Joey, the hours I work are always a problem. If I were to work in an office in downtown Houston, I would have to leave the house at seven in the morning and probably wouldn't get home until seven in the evening. It's best to wait until I get my teaching degree. Then I'll have approximately the same hours and holidays as Joey."

He eyed her consideringly, noting the way she was almost cowering against the wall. What was she afraid of? he wondered. "I can see you've carefully thought out your future."

"I've had to."

"How commendable. Your future should be very bright. And very lonely."

Her body straightened away from the wall in anger. "Rand!"

That was better, he approved silently. "At any rate," he went on smoothly, just as if he hadn't heard the warning in her voice, "I would like to offer you an alternative."

"There isn't one," she replied stonily, thinking of more than just a job.

"There's a vacancy at the clinic now for a bilingual secretary. I assume you took typing in high school?"

"Yes, but my skills are quite rusty."

"Speed would come back. The important thing is that you can translate English into Spanish and Spanish into English. You can, can't you?" His tone was calculated to challenge her.

"Yes!"

"Good. Now your hours would be flexible, according to your needs, and you would easily make twice what you're making now."

"Twice!"

"Maybe three times."

"Rand—"

"And if you're worrying about me being around too much, don't. I'm only there two afternoons a week."

"Rand, it's just not going to work. Can't you accept that?"

"No." Noticing the vulnerable, almost haunted quality that had edged into her eyes, he softened. "At least consider it, Lainie. You would have better working conditions, more interesting work, and a salary that would make things infinitely easier for you. And another thing: Think about that future you're so worried about. You won't always be able to take night courses. Wouldn't it be easier if you had some money set aside so that when the time comes, you could go to school full-time?"

He was talking about a dream she had always had—to be able to devote full time to her studies.

But lately all her dreams had turned to nightmares. Besides, there were just too many negatives to his proposition, and she brought up one of them. "I don't have a car."

"The clinic is on a major bus line."

"I don't have the clothes to work in an office."

"The clinic is very casual. Your jeans and T-shirts would be fine. Remember, our patients come from underprivileged backgrounds."

He made it all sound so simple, Lainie thought, but unfortunately she knew it wasn't. Yet there was the money to consider! Spence hadn't been around for a few days, but she knew better than to think that he had let her completely off the hook. He would be back. If she went to work at the clinic, she could begin saving money, and although she wouldn't be able to offer him anywhere near fifty thousand dollars, it would at least be better than nothing. Surely he would accept some money and leave them alone.

Of course, working at the clinic would blow all to pieces her determination to keep away from Rand. But then they wouldn't be resuming their personal relationship, and he had said himself that he would be working there only two afternoons a week. It stood to reason that during that time he would be busy with patients.

She looked up to find him watching her closely. "Well?"

"I'll have to think about it."

Eight

In the end it wasn't a hard decision to make. Lainie weighed all the pros and cons. Having extra money for herself and Joey didn't come into it at all. She decided she would start a separate bank account into which she would deposit all monies over and above what she was earning now. The money would be saved and used to protect Joey from Spence. And if in the unlikely event Spence disappeared totally from their lives, then the money could be used for Joey, for his college fund and for his future.

The only con she could come up with was having to see Rand twice a week. Obviously that would be the hard part, but then, she reasoned, it couldn't be any harder than *not* seeing him.

The brightly painted clinic was a delight, as were the people who worked in it. It was open every day from ten to six, six days a week, and there was a pool of about thirty doctors and as many nurses who volunteered on a rotating basis, four hours at a time.

Lainie had been nervous about meeting the other workers, but everyone, volunteers and salaried personnel alike, cheerfully welcomed her and eagerly set about putting her at ease and showing her the ropes.

Carla was a tall, sophisticated brunette in her middle thirties. Lainie learned that Carla had once been Rand's Physician's Assistant, but when he decided to start the clinic, he had asked her if she would take the job as its administrator, and now she ran the place with energy and efficiency.

She observed Lainie for a few days, then pronounced herself relieved. "I was so afraid you would be one of those society women who come here trying to impress Rand with their charity, but stay only until they break their first fingernail."

Lainie's mouth dropped open. "You're kidding me. That's really happened?"

"You bet. I've accused Rand more than once of using us down here to screen women for him."

Lainie jumped to his defense before she could think. "He wouldn't do that! He's much too proud of this clinic ever to send anyone here he doesn't think will help it."

Carla looked at her, an expression of understanding beginning to come into her face. "I know. I was just kidding."

A male nurse, Jessie, rescued Lainie from embarrassment. "Don't mind Carla. She's been with Dr. Bennett so long that she tends to act like a mother hen at times. The thing of it is, Dr. Bennett goes his own way no matter what." Jessie shook his head admiringly. "He's so brilliant. Most of the time I think he lives on another planet than us entirely. We just try to stay up, but in general we fail miserably."

Jessie was the clinic's one full-time nurse. He had been a corpsman in Vietnam, and after serving his tour of duty, he had gone to nursing school. He was about five feet ten, with a wiry, muscular build that was deceptively strong. Lainie liked him, and she also liked her new job.

She had her own office. It was small, but it had a nice large window that gave the room plenty of light and warmth. The room was just big enough for a metal desk, a four-drawer file cabinet, and an electric typewriter that struck fear into Lainie's heart the first time she saw it. Gradually, however, her typing skills came back to her, and while she certainly wasn't breaking any records, her accuracy, which had been her strong point in high school, more than made up for any lack of speed.

The thing that she had dreaded most, working in close proximity with Rand, didn't occur her first week at the clinic. But, even though he wasn't physically present, his name was constantly on everyone's lips. From Carla and Jessie right on down to the last volunteer, everyone clearly thought Rand hung both the moon and the stars. Lainie slowly came to the realization that if Carla was the backbone of the clinic, Rand was its heart.

The first afternoon Rand showed up at the clinic, Lainie didn't know what to expect. But by the end of the day when he hadn't singled her out for any special attention, she didn't know whether she should be relieved or upset. She decided she was both.

It was two weeks before he sought her out for a private conversation. Since she typed the schedules, she had known that it was his afternoon to be on duty for the two-to-six shift, but she had it all figured out. She worked nine to five every day. That left only three hours where they might run into each other, and usually she made a point to stay in her office. On this particular afternoon, though, she might as well have saved herself the trouble.

Rand strolled into her office and closed the door as if it were an everyday occurrence. Lainie looked up, startled.

Damn, but she was beautiful, he thought, anger and need stirring in him simultaneously. The anger had become quite a familiar emotion to him. For the first time in his life he was in the position of needing someone who didn't need him, and that made him angry. But his anger wasn't directed at either himself or Lainie, but at the situation between the two of them that he didn't understand.

And of course, there was the need. There had been so many times in the last few weeks when he had known positively he couldn't go one more hour without seeing her. In order to ensure that he keep away from her, he had even flown to Florida for a week to see Rachel and Alex. At the end of the week his two friends had sent him back home with orders to not come back again until either (a) He improved his personality or (b) He brought Lainie with him.

"How are you settling in?" he asked.

"Fine." She automatically flicked the typewriter off. "Everyone who works here is wonderful."

"That's what they say about you." His eyes scanned the office, taking in the new plants in the window, the pictures that were obviously drawn by Joey and held to the side of the file cabinet by brightly colored magnets, and lastly Joey's picture on her desk. "How's Joey?"

"He's doing quite well." *Missing you,* she silently added, *just as I am.* "His arm is in a splint now."

"Good. I'm glad he seems to be healing so well. I was wondering if I could take Joey to a ball game Saturday afternoon. It's between two of the hospital's softball teams, nurses against the laboratory personnel. I think he'd enjoy it."

"I appreciate your asking me here, instead of coming to the house."

He shrugged. "I didn't want to ask you in front of Joey, get his hopes up, and then have you say no."

"That was very considerate of you, because I'm going to have to say no."

"Why?"

"That's something you ask a lot, Rand."

Leaning toward her, his hands came down flat on her desk. "Because I can't accept your decision on any level. Not when my mind tells me there's no rational reason for it, and my body aches night and day for you."

The quick change in his mood and subject matter nearly threw her. "You're talking about an entirely different decision."

Before she could react, he had reached for her and hauled her out of her chair, hard against his body, and crushed his mouth to hers. The kiss was so fast and unexpected, she had no time to erect any defenses. Immediate desire flashed into the lower part of her body, and it was almost shattering. Her head reeled. Kissing Rand was a pleasure forbidden to her. But how could she ever be expected to maintain her defenses against him when every particle of her being clamored for more?

"Stop it, Rand," she gasped.

"Stop what, Lainie? Stop telling you what you already know? Stop making you want me as much as I want you? No way, baby."

She jerked away from him. "I've grown to love this job, Rand. But I'll quit like that"—she snapped her fingers—"if you continue to bother me."

He drew in a rough breath. "Is that what you think I'm doing? Bothering you?"

"Aren't you?"

Cursing fluently, he wheeled and walked to the window. He was so tired of always doing the wrong thing with her. And most important, he was tired of being without her. He felt as if he were going out of his mind. Even his staff had begun to walk very softly around him. Only with his patients and their families had he been able to keep his raw nerves hidden.

Was it remotely possible, he asked himself with despair, that he wouldn't be allowed to have Lainie? *No!* It didn't even bear thinking about. He had known from the first that it wouldn't be easy to win her. If he had to, he would spend the rest of his life trying to get her back.

With his resolve strengthened, he adopted a coolness he didn't even remotely feel and turned back to her. "I don't think asking to take Joey to a ball game is so out of line. I grew very fond of Joey during the time you and I were seeing each other. I miss him, and I don't think I'd be too far off the mark if I said that he misses me too."

"You don't understand, Rand."

Lainie raked her fingers through her hair, and Rand paused to watch as it shimmered back into a straight fall of black around her face. "So you keep telling me. And I'm not liable to understand until you agree to sit down and talk this thing out."

"We did that the other night," she reminded.

"You talked, but mainly I was too stunned to do anything but listen."

Reaction to his presence and to his kiss had begun to set in. Her legs felt too weak to hold her. She sat down. "Leave me alone."

"Impossible."

"Rand . . ." Just for an instant, sorrow overshadowed reason and tears filled her eyes. "Letting you see Joey would have the same potential for disaster as resuming our relationship would!"

"Potential for disaster?"

"What?"

"You said, 'Potential for disaster.' "

Lainie's eyes cleared, and she saw he had gone very still. She could scarcely believe that she had slipped and said what she did.

"What did you mean, Lainie?" he asked softly.

"N-nothing. I guess I just chose—a bad way to

phrase the fact that our relationship can go nowhere, and that there's no need to involve Joey in something that doesn't concern him."

Rand remained silent, studying her. Lainie was a woman who didn't lie. He knew that as well as he knew that the sun would rise tomorrow. Yet something was telling him that she had just lied to him. Was it the first time? he wondered. If she was lying now, she might have lied to him that night when she had said she didn't want to see him again. He had been so bewildered, so thoroughly hurt that night, he wouldn't have been able to tell if she was lying or not. But if she had been, and if she was now, it opened up a whole new set of possibilities that he needed time to think about.

"All right," he murmured. "For now at least I won't try to see Joey."

"Thank you." She was hard pressed to keep the relief out of her voice. If only Spence hadn't seen that picture, she thought, not for the first time. If only he hadn't come back into their lives. But he had, and she was doing the only thing she knew to protect the two people she loved most in the world.

"I was wondering . . . Lainie?"

"Yes?"

"I'm preparing to give a symposium soon, using my knowledge of health problems that are unique to Central America. I'll be teaching American techniques as they can be applied to those problems, and doctors from all over Central America will be coming up to attend."

"It sounds quite interesting," she conceded.

"It's been an interest of mine for quite some time. And since, for health purposes, I've decided to keep away from that geographical area for a while, it's my way of continuing to help the people down there."

His eyes had taken on a slight twinkle, but she had the very sure feeling it hurt him that he could no longer go into Montaraz to treat the people there. She experienced an urge to comfort him. "You do a great deal of good work, Rand, right from this clinic."

"But there's so much left that's undone." He shrugged impatiently. "At any rate I need the talks that I'll be giving transcribed into Spanish."

That would mean working closely with him, Lainie realized, and she knew she wouldn't be able to handle the extra pressure it would put on her. "I'm sorry, Rand, but I can't be away from home any more hours than I already am."

"You won't have to be. You can do the work at home, just like you used to do the sewing, only this won't be a long-term proposition. It should take just a couple of weeks and provide you with added income."

The added income sounded nice, but there was still the problem of being in the position of working even more closely with Rand. "I don't have a type-writer at home."

"I'll lend you one. And if you're worried about having to be too involved with me on this project, don't be. Once I hand over the papers to be trans-lated, you need only contact me if you have a question. And of course, you can take home the Spanish-English medical dictionary that you use here."

He made it all sound so attractive and easy. Did she dare?

"I'd really apprec:~te it, Lainie," he said in a coaxing tone. "My secretary is working on something else for me and doesn't really have the time, and I don't know anyone else to ask."

Dammit! How could a perfectly able man manage to sound so helpless? If she just didn't love him so much. She sighed resignedly. "All right, Rand. When do you want me to start?"

He smiled. "In about a week. I'll let you know. And, Lainie? Thanks."

"God, are you there?" Kneeling in his bedroom by the windowsill, Joey peered intently through the darkness outside his window toward the black night sky high above him. Tonight there weren't even any stars that he could see and direct his prayer toward. *"Things are going awful bad down here. Lainie's working at a place where Rand sometimes works, but she says they hardly see each other. That's not the way it's supposed to be.*

"Remember how I told you that Lainie said Rand asked her to marry him, but that she said no? I guess it's all my fault, because when I prayed that Rand would ask Lainie to marry him, I forgot to say 'Please have her say yes!' Now Lainie's sad, Rosa's upset, and Efrain goes 'round talking to himself. And I never see Rand anymore. I don't understand what's going on. Please, can't you fix it? Can't you help us?" Joey brushed away a stray tear. *"Amen."*

Lainie quietly closed the bedroom door and

slumped against it. How long had this been going on? she wondered, stricken. She had sent him to take a bath and put on his pajamas quite a while ago. Assuming that he had gotten caught up with playing and had forgotten the time, she had decided to check on him and had walked in on his prayer.

Poor little Joey. He had taken all her problems on his own slight shoulders. Lately, of course, Lainie had noticed that he hadn't seemed his usual sunny, carefree self. But after questioning him closely about school and his friends, she had decided it couldn't be anything really important. Having more spare time, not to mention money, she had done special little things with him, believing that his mood was only temporary.

Now she realized it was much more serious than she had imagined. A child's faith was such a very special thing. What would he think when his prayers didn't get answered?

She could never explain to him about Spence. The man was Joey's father. She was sure that as the years went by and Joey grew older, he would discover for himself the type of man his father was. But by then he would be old enough to handle it, old enough to realize that what his father was had very little to do with him. Until that time came, though, she had to continue to shield him from the truth.

Which left her with a dilemma. What should she do? What could she tell him that would allow him to understand and to keep his innocence? That question kept her awake most of the night. By morning she still had no answer.

* * *

Lainie stared unseeing at the keyboard of her typewriter. It was one o'clock in the afternoon, and for the moment anyway, she had lost track of what she was supposed to be working on. It had been that way for the last two days, ever since she had overheard Joey's prayer.

She couldn't tell Rosa about it, much as she would like the older woman's advice, because Rosa didn't understand why she had broken up with Rand either. And Lainie knew that if she told her everything—including Spence's threats—there was no telling what the volatile woman would do.

"Well, now. Fancy this."

Lainie froze as she heard Spence's voice. Her eyes turned toward the door to see him leaning nonchalantly against the doorjamb.

"You know, I have to hand it to you, sweetheart. You actually had me believing that you and the doctor weren't seeing each other, and here all along you've been working for him."

She jumped up. "No, Spence! Please believe me! It's true that I work for his clinic, but we really have broken up. He works here only two afternoons a week, and most of the time I never even see him."

He straightened and sauntered into her office, looking around critically. "And I suppose you expect me to believe that?"

"It's the truth!"

His glance skimmed over Joey's picture and came back to settle on her. "I don't believe you, sweetheart."

She took a deep, calming breath. "It doesn't matter whether you do or not, Spence. The fact of the matter is, there's no way I can come up with the money you want."

"Is that right?"

She pushed her fingers through her hair. "I do have an alternative though. I'm making very good money here, and I can give you part of it. I—"

"Chicken feed!" He almost spit the words out.

"Well, I know, it's not much yet. But give me a few months. Spence! It's all I can do!"

"That's what you think."

"If you're talking about the fifty thousand dollars—"

"I'm not." He turned his head and took a quick look out the door. "You really don't realize what a sweet setup you have here, do you?"

She was confused. "What are you talking about?"

"Drugs, sweetheart, drugs."

"Drugs? Oh, no, Spence!" She began to slowly shake her head. "You can't be thinking what I think you're thinking."

"You always were a smart girl."

"No! There's no way."

"Oh, I admit that it won't bring in the really big bucks I was hoping for. At least, not all at once. But I've done a little research. This clinic is completely self-sufficient in every way. The doctors dispense whatever medications and drugs are necessary right from here so that the people who come here won't have to put out the money for a prescription. All the pharmaceutical companies contribute. There's bound to be quite a lot of drugs here at any one time. So, maybe once a month, you can clean the place out. It's perfect, don't you see? And so simple! You're on the inside. You're the boss's girlfriend. Who's ever gonna suspect you?"

"Spence." Her teeth were clenched together so hard, it almost hurt to say his name. "Forget it right now! I'm not going to steal for you."

"Don't look at it as stealing for me," he advised almost kindly. "Look at it as stealing for the kid. Because that's who will be affected if you don't."

"Even if I were willing, it wouldn't work. There are locks and procedures, Spence."

"Which you know all about."

"I don't have the key, nor do I have access to it, nor will I get it." Her voice was low, trembling.

He lifted his shoulders and waved an innocent hand in the air. "I'm going to give you time to think about this, because I don't believe you're really considering all the possibilities. I'm sure when you realize what the alternative is—"

"Lainie?"

At the sound of Rand's voice, she whirled toward the door.

Puzzled by the look on her face, he switched his gaze to Spence. "I'm sorry, I didn't mean to interrupt. I didn't realize Lainie had anyone in her office." He offered his hand. "I'm Rand Bennett."

Suddenly Spence was all glittering charm. "Dr. Bennett, it's such a pleasure to finally meet you! Lainie mentions you often."

Rand's eyebrow flew up. "Oh?"

"Well, gosh darn, I apologize. I haven't introduced myself yet, have I? And Lainie always was a little lax where manners were concerned."

Rand's voice dropped several degrees in temperature. "I've always found Lainie's manners to be perfect."

"Well, of course," Spence came back, smooth as oiled glass. "She's great and all self-taught. Her mother really fell down on the job."

Turning away to the window, Lainie bit down hard on her lip. Spence knew that she wouldn't contradict him in front of Rand. And added to that she realized that the less she said in front of Rand, the better.

"At any rate"—Spence affably offered his hand—"I'm Spence Gordon."

"Joey's father?"

"That's right. I'm mighty proud of that little fellow. We're close as two peas in a pod, he and I."

Rand eyed the man in front of him throughtfully. There was something going on here, and he intended to find out what it was. "You must have really been worried the day Joey was hit by that car."

Spence started visibly. "Car?"

"It was just fortunate that he wasn't hurt any worse, wasn't it?"

"*Yes!* Oh, absolutely. That's just what I was telling Lainie. Lainie, sweetheart"—she felt his fingers curl around her upper arm, and she only just managed not to shudder—"I've got to be going now. But you give Joey a big kiss for me and tell him I'll be seeing him real soon. And I'll talk to you in a day or so. In the meantime you think over what we were discussing."

Lainie nodded dully, and Rand stepped aside so that the older man could leave. "It was nice meeting you."

"Yes sir! It was nice meeting you, too, Dr. Bennett. Perhaps we'll be seeing each other in the near future."

"Perhaps." Rand watched Spence Gordon leave, then looked back at Lainie. She still looked as pale as she had when he had first walked in. "Are you all right?" he asked quietly.

She moistened her lips and sat down in her desk chair. "I'm fine. Was there something you wanted?"

He glanced down at the file in his hand. "I have a patient here who is going back home to Mexico. I've written a letter to his doctor there, advising him of the patient's condition. I'd like you to type it."

"No problem." Lainie took the file and flipped it open to the letter Rand had written in longhand. He had written it in part English, part Spanish. Her job would be to transcribe the whole letter into Spanish. She had done similar letters for two of the other doctors, and she was finding that it was getting easier and easier for her.

"Lainie?"

She looked up to find him frowning.

"Are you really all right?"

"Sure. Why wouldn't I be?"

"Spence Gordon didn't even know Joey had had an accident, did he?"

She almost flinched at his perception. "No. He, uh, hasn't been around for a while. I'll do this letter right away. Is there anything else?"

He stared at her for a moment longer. "No. I guess not."

Nine

Lainie was living on sheer nerves. Every time the phone rang, she would cringe. Every time someone knocked on the front door, she would jump. Efrain offered her her old job back, thinking that the new one was too hard on her. Rosa brought food, deciding that she wasn't eating enough.

It was their contention that she was ill, and Lainie wasn't sure that they weren't right. Certainly the dark circles under her eyes seemed to bear out their theory. But while Lainie appreciated their concern, she wasn't sure that treating the symptoms was going to do any good. Because, when all was said and done, the cause could not be changed.

Rand seemed as if he were there every time she turned around, creating opportunities to talk with her, to touch her, and in general making her life more difficult.

Joey, bless his heart, began trying to make deals in his nightly conversations with God. One night Lainie overheard him saying, *"I promise I'll keep my room cleaner if you'll just make Lainie happy again."*

Lainie didn't get much sleep that night. But then she wasn't sleeping a lot anyway. She came to the conclusion that it was the little things—a smile, a touch, a word, a prayer—that might be her undoing in the end. It was just like life. The little things wore a person down, day after day, until—when something major happened—a person had no strength left to draw upon. Lainie began to wonder if she would have the fortitude to go on.

One morning, about a week after Spence had visited her at the clinic and given her his new demands, the phone rang. Joey had already left for school, and she was on her way out the door heading for work. She stared undecidedly at the phone, tempted to let it go unanswered, but it continued to ring. She gave in and went to answer it.

"Hello?"

"Lainie? Oh, great, I got you before you left."

"Carla? Is anything wrong? You sound awful."

"I feel terrible. I woke up this morning with some kind of bug, and I'm not going to be able to come in to work this morning."

"Of course not!" Lainie exclaimed sympathetically. "The way you sound, you belong in bed today."

"I'm afraid you're right, and that's just where I'm

headed as soon as I get off the phone. The thing is, that leaves us a problem with the keys."

"Keys?" Lainie felt as if she had just been given a transfusion of ice water. Her whole body went cold.

"The keys to the front door and to the drug area. You'll need them to open up. Could you possibly run by my house and pick them up on your way to the clinic?"

"No! I—I mean, I don't have a car. I ride the bus to work."

"Oh, shoot. That's right. I knew that. This virus has affected my brain. Uh, let me think. . . . I've got it! How long will it take you to get to the clinic?"

Lainie consulted her watch. "If I walk out the door within the next five minutes, I can catch the eight-thirty bus, and that lets me out on the corner by the clinic about ten to nine."

"Great. I'll have my husband waiting for you, and he can give you the keys."

Lainie didn't want any part of the keys. She had told Spence there was no way she could get hold of them, and here they were practically being forced on her, no questions asked. If it weren't so sad, she would have laughed. She just wasn't going to get a break.

She wished fervently that she could tell Carla she couldn't possibly take responsibility for the keys, but she knew she couldn't do that. Carla needed her help.

"Fine," Lainie said, more firmly than she felt. "That will be fine. And Carla, I hope you get well fast."

"I will," Carla assured. "I have a great constitution. I'll go to bed and sleep it off, and by tomorrow I'm sure I'll be as good as new."

"I hope so," Lainie murmured, and hung up the phone, then saying to herself, "For more reasons than one."

The day didn't go well. For one thing the clinic was unusually busy, and with Carla out, Lainie pitched in and helped wherever she could.

Then at three o'clock Spence called.

Hearing his voice, her heart began to hammer so loudly, she was surprised he didn't hear it through the phone and comment on it. "What do you want, Spence?"

He didn't waste time with his usual preliminaries. "The key." It flashed through her mind to wonder if he had ESP, but his next words told her he didn't. "Have you figured out how to get your hands on it and the drugs yet?"

Relief that he didn't know she had the key to the drug area made her voice strong. "I told you that there's no way!" The next instant, though, she decided that she might as well have saved her breath.

"You know the old saying," he growled. " 'Where there's a will, there's a way.' Maybe, sweetheart, the trouble is that your will just isn't strong enough. But don't worry. I'm about to fix that. I'm going to give you until tomorrow at this time. If at that time you don't have either drugs or money to turn over to me . . . well"—he gave a particularly unpleasant laugh—"let me just suggest it would be in your best interest, and Joey's, to have one or the other."

Lainie hung up the phone and let her head fall into her hands. *I can handle Spence. I can handle Spence.* She kept repeating the phrase over the corner. Another doctor had taken the afternoon shift, so she hadn't expected to see him. herself. She had Joey today, and she would have him tomorrow. The day after tomorrow . . . maybe Spence would just go away. She spent several minutes trying to convince herself of that, then gave up. Realistically she wasn't sure of anything anymore, including whether she could take one more ounce of pressure—from anyone or anything.

By five forty-five that afternoon thunder was rumbling ominously overhead. Lainie sat glumly at her desk. She had already called Rosa to tell her that she would be late, because she needed to stay at the clinic until six to close up.

She had thought briefly about giving the keys to Jessie so that he could close up and take them home with him. But because the keys had been entrusted to her, and because Spence wanted her to use them to steal, she had obstinately decided that she would take on the sole responsibility for them, guard them to the best of her ability, and turn them back over to Carla completely intact, along with the contents of the drug room. No doubt, she pondered crossly, it was a stupid way to look at the matter, and no doubt the decision would make her lose sleep tonight.

It would also probably get her very wet. She gazed out the window at the angry sky and made a bet with herself that it would begin to rain within the next fifteen minutes—just about the time when she would be standing on the corner waiting for the bus. Oh, well, the day was nearly over, she decided philosophically. Not much else could happen.

She was wrong again.

Rand strolled in and settled himself on the edge of her desk, one leg on the floor, one leg hooked over the corner. Another doctor had taken the afternoon shift, so she hadn't expected to see him. Her voice reflected her surprise. "Hi, what are you doing here?"

"I called here earlier in the day and spoke to Jessie. He told me you were going to stay an extra hour so that you could lock up. I just wanted to tell you how much I appreciate your stepping in for Carla today."

Her gaze strayed to his beautiful long-fingered hands linked loosely together. If only she didn't remember how thrillingly they had once stroked her body. *No.* She stopped herself. She couldn't think that way and still remain sane. She forced herself to relax. "I was glad to do anything I could to help. Besides, I haven't done that much."

"That's not what Jessie says. He says you've been right in there today, pitching in where you were needed, making sure that everything ran smoothly."

"Thanks." Rand's praise warmed her. There were times when she felt so alone, so forlorn, that it was good to hear someone tell her she was doing something right.

Suddenly Rand gave a great laugh as he spied a

drawing held to the side of her file cabinet by a heart-shaped magnet. "What's that?"

Glancing over her shoulder toward the large rectangular-shaped sheet of manila paper, she chuckled. "You mean, you can't tell what that is?"

Rand peered closer. "Well, it's obviously a stick figure, and hanging around its neck is something that could very well be a snake with a large head."

"Rand! I can't believe you don't recognize a stethoscope when you see one."

"A stethoscope. Ah-ha! Then that explains why it has 'Dr. Joey Gordon' scrawled above it in vivid red crayon."

She laughed, her first real laugh in a long time. "You knew what it was all along."

"Absolutely. Joey obviously has real talent. That's a superior rendering of a doctor if I ever saw one."

"Yes, that's just what I thought." It felt good to be laughing with Rand, she reflected. She had missed it.

"At a guess I would say he has decided he wants to become a doctor."

"That's right." She shook her head. "It's been a little hard on all of us. Rosa, Efrain, myself—none of us has been safe."

"Been practicing on you, has he?"

"I'm afraid so. And do you remember Bunny Bear?"

"I sure do."

"He's gotten the worst of it. Joey decided that one of Bunny Bear's arms was broken and needed a cast."

"What happened? Did Bunny Bear run out into the street and get hit by a car?"

"Something like that," she agreed ruefully. "And the closest Joey could come to a cast in our kitchen—Emergency Room was to make one out of flour and water."

Rand's eyes brimmed with mirth. "Don't tell me!"

"He papier-mâchéd Bunny Bear's arm. Now I'm afraid that when Dr. Joey decides that the arm is healed and he takes the cast off, fur and all will come off."

"I wouldn't worry about it too much. Bunny Bear looked plenty tough to me."

"Yeah, well, he's sort of had to be."

Jessie stuck his head in the door. "Hey, Dr. Bennett! I didn't know you were here."

"I haven't been here long. I thought I would drop by and offer Lainie a ride home."

"Good idea. That way she won't have to stand out in the rain and wait for the bus."

Rand stood up, walked to the window, and looked out. "I doubt if it's going to rain. I just thought that since she worked an extra hour this evening, I'd save her that long bus ride home."

Jessie grinned. "Whatever you say. Lainie, here's the keys." He tossed them to her and she caught them neatly. "Carla called earlier and said that she's feeling a lot better, and that she'd meet you in the morning in front of the clinic and you can give her the keys then."

Her hand closed tightly around the keys, the only sign of the tension that had begun to build inside her the moment Rand had said he intended to take her home. "Thanks, Jessie."

"Sure." He glanced uncertainly at Rand. "Can I do anything for you before I leave?"

"Not a thing. Have a nice evening, Jessie."

"Thanks. See you in the morning, Lainie."

"Bye." She waited until Jessie left. "Rand, I'm perfectly capable of taking the bus home."

"I know," he said easily. "It's just that I thought tonight would be a perfect time to run over to my house and pick up the papers I want you to type."

"Why couldn't you have brought them here?" she asked suspiciously.

"I came straight from the hospital. Besides, the typewriter is at my house too." He paused. "Are you afraid to come to my house with me?"

Now how could she answer that? she wondered. Afraid? Absolutely! "I just don't see the point," she finally answered. "Couldn't you bring them by here tomorrow?"

"I could," he agreed. "But how are you going to lug the typewriter home on the bus?"

"Well . . ."

"Lainie, sooner or later, I'll have to bring the typewriter to you. It might as well be tonight, don't you think? I'm eager for you to get started on these papers."

She chewed on her bottom lip. "Is it important that they're done soon?"

"Not that soon. But I don't want you to be rushed, and I figure if you work on them an hour or so every night, you'll have them all ready by the time of my symposium."

It sounded reasonable. So reasonable in fact, she

couldn't think of a logical rebuttal. "All right. Let me call Rosa and tell her I'm going to be even later than I thought."

"Why don't I call Rosa while you go check and make sure everything's closed up? I'd like to say hello to her."

She shrugged. "Okay. Tell her I shouldn't be too long."

As Rand pulled his car under the side portico of his house, the sound of the rain drumming against the car ceased. Switching off the ignition of the car, he arched an eyebrow in disgust at the rain that was coming down in heavy sheets off the portico roof.

"The people at the hospital may be in awe of that eyebrow of yours, but I doubt if it will hold much sway with the rain," Lainie commented, unable to resist.

He lay his arm along the back of the seat and looked at her. It was so nice to have her this close to him, he reflected, just as it was so nice to have her teasing him again. "I suppose you knew all along it was going to rain?"

She grinned. "Well, actually . . . yes."

"How do you know so much about the weather?"

"Rand! Clouds have been rolling in for most of the day. The sky has been darkening. It was thundering for heaven's sake! Why wouldn't I know it was going to rain?"

He longed to pick up a lock of her hair and stroke it to see if it was really as silky as he remembered, but he didn't want to put her on the defensive. Not yet at any rate. "I didn't."

Her lips twitched in amusement. "Jessie's right. You do live on your own planet."

He stared at her blankly for a moment, then smiled. "I'm afraid he's probably right—under certain circumstances and at certain times."

"Like today?" she asked, still kidding.

"Like lately. I've been very single-minded. There's been only you on my mind."

Her heart jumped, then began beating irregularly. Damn! She couldn't let his sudden change of moods affect her so! "That's too bad. It's such a waste of time."

"I suppose that's for me to decide, don't you?"

"Look, why don't you go get the papers and the typewriter," she suggested cooly, trying not to betray her nervousness, "and I'll wait here."

"No, no, no!" He grabbed her arm, opened his door, and began pulling her across the seat, all at practically the same time. "You can't sit out here. Haven't you noticed? It's raining!"

"This is an amazing house," Lainie murmured, still a bit dazed that she was even in the house. "It appears to be perfectly run, but I never see anyone running it."

"I pay people a lot of money so that they'll disappear at the appropriate times."

"Mmm." This whole situation, she reflected, was entirely too volatile. They needed to get out of here as soon as possible. "Where are the papers?"

He motioned with his arm. "This way."

A minute later she was standing in the middle of his study, admiring it. She had never been in this particular room before, but she guessed that this was a room Rand would spend a lot of time in, and she wanted to explore it. Sneaking a look in his direction, she saw that he was occupied at his desk, sorting through some papers, so she let her feet take a meandering course around the study.

The room contained no central overhead light, but Rand had switched on several lamps. The day outside had darkened into a stormy evening, and inside the room had taken on a cozy, amber glow.

Books decorated the walls in tall, custom-built shelves. By the big bay window she found a giant globe. She ran her hands across the smooth marble of the fireplace, let one hand trail over the soft suede of an armchair, then snaked the pad of one finger down the spine of a leather-bound book. With its warmth, intelligence, and sensuality the room personified Rand.

Her eyes cut to him and found him watching her. The papers he had been sorting through were in the exact position as they had been the last time she had looked.

"You know, late one night not too long after I met you, I sat here in this room and thought about you and how your presence would make my house into a home."

His voice contained that deeply mesmerizing quality she had noticed for the first time when he had talked a fearful Joey through a shot. She remembered at the time thinking how easily he could catch a person unawares if they weren't careful. "Rand, please, don't."

"And then I called some friends of mine and told them I had found the woman I was going to marry."

"The way things have turned out, that was a bit foolish, don't you think?"

"No. I haven't given up."

"You should."

"I can't."

His quiet determination sent cold chills up her spine. "Get the papers and take me home," she ordered.

He rose and slowly made his way around the desk. "Hasn't it occurred to you yet? You're trapped here until I decide to take you home."

She stood her ground, refusing to back away from him or show him that she was affected in any way. "Rand, you can't keep me here."

"I think I can," he corrected quite gently.

"Rosa will wonder—"

"I told her not to expect you until quite, quite late." He stopped right in front of her.

"But Joey—"

"She said she'd take care of him."

"You had no right!" Her jade eyes hardened in anger, but her anger made no impression on him.

"Actually I did worse than that," he returned evenly. "I told her that you wouldn't be coming home until morning and to please keep him overnight. By the way, she said she'd be delighted to."

"What do you expect to gain by doing this?" For the first time, she realized that she had begun to tremble, and she wondered when the trembling had started.

"Gain? Maybe a little peace of mind, maybe the truth, maybe surcease."

"You're just used to getting your way," she charged heatedly.

"Maybe I was before you came into my life, but all of that has certainly come to a screeching halt, wouldn't you agree?"

Quite casually his hand slid into her hair so that his fingers cupped her head and his thumb was in the position to trace the sensitive edge of her ear. Her mind told her to move, but her body told her to stay.

"Please don't do this, Rand."

"All right." His head lowered until she could feel his breath against her lips. "If you'll tell me you don't want me to, I'll stop."

"I don't want you to." She ignored the breathlessness she heard in her voice and decided that her words should certainly be clear enough for anyone.

"And say it like you mean it," he added softly, but roughly. His tongue touched her mouth and began lazily to outline the shape, then carefully drew its way down the center, probing, until involuntarily her lips parted, and she could feel the warmth of his breath inside her. Passion flowered and flowed to all her extremities.

"I don't want—"

His tongue thrust deeply into her mouth, and his hand slipped beneath her sweater to glide across her back. She felt her skin flush, then catch on fire.

"Convince me, Lainie." His words were spoken barely above a whisper, but she heard them.

"I don't—" He pulled her tightly to him. His hand closed over her breast, and a thumb flicked over her nipple. "I—"

"Shut up, Lainie," he muttered. "Just shut up." His mouth crushed into hers, and the world narrowed to just her and Rand.

His name was ringing in her head—*Rand, Rand, Rand*—and she couldn't be sure, but it seemed as though she was repeating it over and over. But how could that be? When his lips were kissing her so thoroughly, and his hands were lifting her sweater up and over her head. And then they were sinking together to the floor.

A desperate need was pounding through Rand. All patience had gone, all gentleness had fled. He wanted her fiercely and that's the way he would make love to her.

She made no demur. His body was transmitting its urgency to her, and she eagerly helped him to undress her and after that him.

It had been so long since she had touched him, so long since he had touched her. Their flesh hungered, and their love poured out, manifesting itself in kisses that seemed without end and caresses that were surely capable of causing madness. Her long black hair twined around them. Under her hands, his muscles tensed; under his hands, she softened and flowed. Each of them trembled equally.

Finally neither of them could take it one second longer. She caught his muscled buttocks with her hands, urging him into her. He groaned, swore, and called out her name. Gone were her fears.

Gone was his pain. Their passion had consumed it all.

Together they fitted perfectly; together they made one. Outside the rain came down, and inside, their fire raged out of control, not quickly or easily put out.

Ten

Lainie stood at a window of Rand's bedroom. The rain had nearly stopped. Soon the new day would begin. Pulling the lapels of his bathrobe closer around her, she glanced toward him. He was sleeping deeply, his breathing slow and steady. Even though he didn't show the obvious physical signs as she did, she had the distinct impression he had lost just as much sleep as she had over the last few weeks.

The truth was, they had both been through hell, and it wasn't over yet. She looked around for her purse and located it on his dresser. Although she was vague about the exact time they had come to bed, she could remember hours before how they had lain on the plush carpet of the study's floor, calculating the chances of their having strength enough to pick up their clothes and walk to his bedroom. Holding each other tightly, they had laughed and decided they wouldn't make it. Then they had made love again, dozed a little, and finally concluded they simply had to try anyway, because they were getting so stiff from lying on the floor, they were afraid their joints might lock. Scooping up their clothes, they took a detour by the kitchen to pick up some food, and at last managed to make it to his bedroom. They had eaten, made love some more, and fallen asleep.

Except Lainie hadn't been able to sleep too long, because she still had Spence to contend with. He had said he would be in touch with her today at three. She zipped open her purse, delved into it, and came out with the keys. She lay them on her outstretched palm and gazed at them.

If it ever came down to an actual choice between being able to keep Joey and stealing drugs, Lainie knew she would steal the drugs. She would murder to keep Joey, she told herself. But it wasn't going to come to that.

Because sometime during the night of love that had just passed, things had crystallized in her mind. Up until now, she had been able to protect Rand and Joey. But, the problem was, they were all miserable and Spence was still ever-present. She had made up her mind. Once and for all she was going to end the demands Spence had been making on her. If all went as she planned, Spence would be out of their lives by tonight.

Slowly her palm closed over the keys and tightened. She didn't notice their sharp edges biting into her skin until she heard Rand stir behind her.

"Lainie?"

She let the keys fall back into her purse and turned around. Her mouth curved tenderly. "Hi."

"Hi, yourself." He grinned sleepily and held out his hand. "Come back to bed."

Without a word she slipped in beside him. He rubbed his hand over the thick terry of his robe. "Are you warm enough."

"Mmm-hmm."

He kissed the baby-soft skin at her temple. "Why couldn't you sleep? Is something bothering you?"

"No. Really, not a thing."

She had said it too fast, averted her eyes too quickly, he thought. She wasn't telling him the truth, and it hurt like hell. His finger lightly stroked her collarbone. "I've been worried about you, Lainie. Look at you. You've lost weight. You have dark shadows under your eyes." He gently touched the delicate skin he had just spoken of.

"I look pretty bad, huh?"

"I'm not going to let you make this into a joke. I'm worried about you. I know something's wrong, and it's driving me crazy that you won't confide in me."

He hadn't really thought that tricking her into spending one night with him would solve all their problems, but he had hoped it would be a good start toward tearing down the barriers that had been between them these last weeks. The difficulty was, he hadn't understood the barriers then, and he didn't understand them now. How could he fight something she wouldn't talk to him about?

A finger under her chin forced her face up so that he could see her eyes. "Lainie," he said very carefully. "You can accuse me of being arrogant or overbearing or anything else you want, but I'm telling you now, if you think for one minute I'm going to let you out that bedroom door over there without a solemn promise from you that you will marry me, you're very much mistaken. I'm perfectly capable of keeping you a prisoner here for the rest of your natural life if necessary."

"A prisoner! Would you really do that, Rand?"

"Absolutely." The tiny shards of humor within the jade depths of her eyes made him feel a little better. "Lainie, do you know the odds against you and me finding each other at all? They must be astronomical. But we did. We came together, fell in love, and it was wonderful. Then for some reason we had to part. I won't allow that to happen again. So let me hear you say it," he demanded. "Let me hear you say you'll marry me."

"I—I can't."

"Lainie." His voice held a caution. "I wasn't kidding about keeping you here."

"I can't tell you what you want to hear right now. You're going to have to bear with me just a little while longer."

"Bear with you? What are you talking about?"

"I can't explain. I'm sorry. I wish I could. I wish things were different."

He brushed a strand of hair away from her face. "Lainie, you're scaring me."

"No!" She gently caressed his cheek. "Oh, no. I don't mean to. Let me have until tonight. Tonight I'm hoping I'll be able to give you the answer you want."

His forehead creased. "Lainie, you can't expect me to be satisfied with that. Why can't you tell me now? What's going to happen between now and tonight?"

"Rand"—she cast about in her mind for something that would make him accept what she was demanding of him a little easier—"I tell you what. Come pick me up at the clinic at five-thirty."

"Five-thirty?" He frowned. "That's later than when you usually leave."

"No questions, Rand! Please!" She threaded her fingers through his hair. "Now, since five-thirty this afternoon is such a long way off, and since it's not yet six this morning, why don't we"—she darted her tongue into his ear—"make love?"

"Lainie, don't do that! I can't think when you do that." Her hand began to smooth down his abdomen, but he was grimly determined. *"I want to talk about this."*

"Please, Rand," she whispered. "I need you."

"Dammit, Lainie. Stop it!"

She had learned her strength. "No."

Rand had to leave before she did, but he arranged for a cab to pick her up and take her to the clinic. He also extracted a firm promise from her that she *would* be waiting for him at the clinic at five-thirty.

Lainie showered, called Joey and wished him a good morning, then literally bit her nails until it was time to go to the clinic. Once there her anxiety over her upcoming confrontation with Spence didn't improve. The one bright spot in the day occurred early on when, with great relief, she was able to hand the keys back over to Carla.

Unfortunately it was an unusually slow day, giving her plenty of time to think of everything that could go wrong with her plan. As the day went on, her nerves wound tighter and tighter until she had to give up all pretense of working and just sit and wait.

Finally, with every sign of supreme confidence and expectation, Spence strolled into her office at three o'clock. Leaning his hips back against her desk, he folded his arms across his chest and raised his eyebrows at her in a silent question.

The gesture didn't faze her. She had seen it done by the best. Besides, she was long since past the stage of being afraid. She was not going to allow herself to fail. Deciding to go on the offensive right away, she greeted him coolly with a nod. "This is where I work. I would have preferred it if you had called, and we could have arranged for some place to meet."

"What you would prefer, sweetheart, doesn't enter into this. I told you that you had until today, and I'm tired of screwing around with you. What have you decided? Is it going to be drugs? Or money? Or do I get to play Daddy with Joey?"

She stood up so that she would be on eye level with him. "It's going to be none of those things."

He jerked up from the desk. "What?"

"You heard me. None of those choices is acceptable. You see, Spence, I've done some thinking and come to some decisions." Her hands were clenched inside the pockets of her skirt. "And the first decision I've made is that I'm going to the police."

Spence's mouth fell open, momentarily showing his shock. However, he recovered quickly, and his face creased into a slow smile. "I don't believe you. You're bluffing."

"No, Spence, I'm not. I'm tired of you harassing me and threatening Joey."

He shrugged innocently. "What harassing? What threatening? I'm just a father worried about his son."

"I think you'd better practice the delivery of your lines, Spence. You're not a very good actor, and you're going to have to give an Academy Award performance if you want the judge to believe you."

"Judge?"

"I'm taking you to court to get legal custody of Joey."

"And just where are you going to get the money?" He smirked. "Have you suddenly decided to abandon your scruples and ask your boyfriend for money? It's about time. After all, why shouldn't he pay for what he's been getting for free all this time? And, since you've decided to get his money anyway, we might as well work together on this. We'll eliminate the middleman. There's no sense in lawyers getting any money when we can keep it in the family. You give the money to me, and you can have the kid."

"I'm going to go through Legal Aid," she said steadily. "Rand doesn't come into this."

His eyes went as hard as flint. "There's no way you'll win. You don't stand a chance."

That he might be right scared her to death, but she wasn't going to back down. "I think I will. Why would anyone give custody of a child to a man who, in the last four years, hasn't even tried to see his son or spend time with him, much less get him back?"

"I've had a change of heart," he retorted slyly. "People can change. I can convince the judge of that."

Lainie was reminded that she was dealing with an expert at the art of conning. "Maybe, maybe not," she returned noncommittally. "But tell me, Spence, what are you going to tell him when he asks what you do to make a living?"

He lifted his shoulders unconcernedly. "A little of this, a little of that."

"But *exactly* what? Since you lost the job as pilot for that commuter airline, what have you been doing? I wouldn't imagine there's too much call these days for second-rate alcoholic pilots."

He pointed a rigid finger at her, and his face reddened in anger. "Listen to me, little girl. I make good money. You don't have to worry about that. I can support Joey."

"So can I. But I can also tell the judge precisely what I do. He can talk with the people I work with. He can visit the building I work in. He can see the stubs of my salary checks. He can look at my income tax returns." She paused and met his eyes squarely. "Can you say the same thing?"

His gaze faltered first. "If you must know, I fly for a small private air-freight service. We have international contracts. But I repeat, you're bluffing!"

"I wouldn't count on it, Spence." Her heart sank at the disclosure of his new employment. Yet she had set her course, and she intended to follow through with it. Too much depended on the outcome. "Besides, even if what you say is true about your job, I still have a feeling that your life-style won't bear too much scrutiny. And there's always the little matter of blackmail."

"I'd be careful of what I said if I were you," he sneered menacingly. "Blackmail is an ugly word."

She spoke very distinctly. "But then, Spence, you're an ugly man."

For a moment she thought he was going to hit her, but he visibly pulled himself together. "You've got no proof."

"How do you know what I have and don't have?"

His control snapped, and he yanked her to him and began to shake her violently. "Now, you listen to me, you little—"

"No! You listen to me!"

Suddenly Lainie was free and gazing at a Rand she had never seen before. He was absolutely livid. Every muscle in his body was coiled, ready for battle. He had grabbed the front of the man's shirt in his hand, pulling Spence right up to him and almost choking him in the process. "Suppose you tell me what you thought you were doing by laying one slimy finger on Lainie?" His voice was dangerously quiet, but a vein beat furiously in his temple.

"How long have you been there?" Spence managed to gasp out.

"Long enough. Talk!"

Spence pulled frantically at Rand's hands, trying to get him to loosen his hold. "We were just having a little family disagreement. That's all." He tried to look over his shoulder to Lainie. "Tell him."

"Rand, let him go."

He didn't look at her. "How long has he been blackmailing you?"

She sighed, rubbing her hand across her fore-head. "Quite a while."

"Since before you told me you didn't want to see me anymore?"

"Yes,"she admitted.

Rand released Spence by shoving him hard against the file cabinet. "The light dawns."

She went to his side. "Try to understand. I did what I thought was best to protect both you and Joey. I never meant to hurt you."

Rand's arm came around her. "I do understand, Lainie. And I love you for trying to protect me. I just wish you would have had more faith in my ability to help you."

His eyes cut to Spence, who had straightened away from the file cabinet. "I heard you say you were flying for a private freight service. Is that right?"

Spence eyed him warily. "Yes."

"And would I be right in guessing that those international contracts you were so busy bragging about are for Central and South American routes?"

"Yes."

"You know, I can't help but find that very inter-esting. And what *you* might find interesting is that I have excellent connections in Central and South America. At my request a network of information—from both sides of the law—is instantly available to me." He noticed with satis-faction that Spence's ruddy complexion had lost its color. "Now it occurs to me that such a freight service would be a terrific cover for someone flying controlled substances in and out of those areas.

Uh, are you with me so far?" Spence returned his look with hate. "Good. Now, what I want you to do is give me an address where you will be at ten o'clock tomorrow morning. My lawyer will be by at that time with papers that state you are turning over legal guardianship of Joey to Lainie. You, Spence, will sign those papers."

Spence slanted a calculating look at Lainie. "Why should I?"

"Because," Rand said quite gently, "I can have you thrown into any South American jail I wish for as long as I choose. And, just in case you're in doubt, let me tell you that I will choose the jail where the conditions are the worst and that you will be in there so long, that your bones will be rotted before it's time for you to get out."

"But what if I'm not guilty?"

"It won't matter."

Spence's eyes were filled with pure venom. He grabbed up a piece of paper, scribbled his address, and thrust it at Lainie. "Here." He wheeled to go, but the sound of Rand's voice momentarily halted him.

"Ten o'clock, Spence. Be there. And one more thing. If at any time you are tempted to contact either Lainie or Joey, just remember that it would be extremely unwise, not to mention dangerously bad for your health." Rand smiled, not kindly. "I'm a doctor. I know about these things."

Spence stalked out, and Lainie let out a long breath of relief. She couldn't believe it! It was all over! But then again, was it? Raising concerned eyes to Rand, she asked, "Can you forgive me?"

"Lainie! There's nothing to forgive. I'm just sorry

that you had to go through this all alone." He drew her close. "You know, there's one thing you're going to have to learn about me. Just because I'm a surgeon of some skill doesn't mean that I need to be kept in a rarefied bubble, protected from the realities of life. My everyday life *is* reality. It *is* life and death. And I'm very good at my job."

She smiled. "I see that now."

Cradling her face between his two hands, he murmured, "I'm so proud of you and what you did. You were very brave. But just remember for the future: You don't have to be brave alone. Between us we're going to be able to handle anything that life throws our way. Do you believe that?"

She nodded, tears misting her eyes. "There's something else you should know. You and I haven't been the only ones affected by all this."

"What do you mean?"

"It's Joey. I'm afraid that we've been the subject of all his prayers lately. By accident I overheard him one night. He was taking all the blame for everything that was going wrong between us."

"But why?"

"It seems he asked God to have you propose to me, but he forgot to mention to God that He should arrange to have me say yes."

"Poor little guy. He must have been having a real hard time."

Lainie shook her head. "I hurt so bad for him, Rand, but I couldn't explain to him what was going on."

"Don't worry. We'll make it up to him." Rand grinned mischievously. "And for his prayers, he gets my undying gratitude. Remind me to buy him a car tomorrow. What kind do you think he'd like?"

"A car!" She looked up at him. "Rand, you can't be serious."

"Lainie, Lainie, where's your faith? I was talking about a Hot Wheel."

"Okay." Her eyes glittered with happiness, but she placed her hands on her hips in mock challenge. "Speaking of faith, or lack of it, why are you here early? By any chance did you doubt that I would be here when I said I would be?"

He arched his one brow. "I think we've talked enough. Come here." And he drew her into his arms for a long, deep kiss.

"Hi, God. It's me again, Joey. I just wanted to tell you that everything has turned out great! Lainie and Rand were married yesterday. It was in the church with flowers and candles and everything. Lainie had this fancy white dress with a skirt so long, she had to have someone help her walk. God, I never saw anyone look so beautiful. Rand must have thought so too, because he had tears in his eyes when he saw Lainie walking down the aisle toward him.

"And then there was the reception! You've never tasted such good food!" He glanced uncertainly toward the ceiling. *"If you like food, that is. Anyway, now Rand's taken her to some island—I can't say the name of it the right way—for their honeymoon. A honeymoon"*—he paused to explain—*"is a name for a trip so they can be alone. I don't mind at all. I'm staying with Rosa*

and Efrain. When Lainie and Rand come back, we're all going to live in Rand's big house. It's real neat. It has its own park and a pool with fancy fish, and Lainie says she won't have to sleep on the sofa anymore.

"Anyway, I just wanted to say thanks." He peeked upwards through the thickness of his lashes and added brightly, "And if there's ever anything I can do to help you, just let me know. Amen."

THE EDITOR'S CORNER

If there were a theme for next month's LOVESWEPT romances, it might be "Pennies from Heaven," because in all four books something wonderful seems to drop from above right into the lives of our heroes or heroines.

First, in Peggy Webb's utterly charming **DONOVAN'S ANGEL**, LOVESWEPT #143, Martie Fleming tumbles down (literally) into Paul Donovan's garden. Immediately fascinated by Martie, Paul feels she is indeed a blessing straight from heaven—an especially appropriate notion as he's a minister. But, discovering his vocation, Martie runs for cover, convinced that she is so unconventional she could never be a clergyman's wife. Most of the parishioners seem to agree: her spicy wit and way-out clothes and unusual occupation set their tongues wagging. Paul, determined as he is to have Martie, seems fated to lose . . . until a small miracle or two intervenes. You simply can't let yourself miss this funny, heartwarming love story that so perfectly captures the atmosphere of a small Southern town.

The very title of our next romance, **WILD BLUE YONDER**, LOVESWEPT #144, by Millie Grey, gives you a clue to how it fits our theme. Mike Donahue pilots an antique biplane like a barnstormer of years gone by. And when he develops engine trouble and lands on Krissa Colbrook's property, he's soon devel-

(continued)

oping trouble for her too . . . trouble of the heart. The last kind of man placid Krissa needs or wants in her life is a daredevil, yet she falls hard for this irresistible vagabond who's come to her from the sky above. We think it would be hard for a reader to fail to be charmed by Mike, so we feel secure in saying that you will be enchanted by the way Mike goes about ridding Krissa of her fears!

For just a second now try to put yourself into the very large shoes of one Morgan Abbott, hero of talented newcomer Linda Cajio's **ALL IS FAIR . . .**, LOVESWEPT #145. Imagine that you (you're that handsome Morgan, remember?) are having dinner with acquaintances when an absolutely stunning beauty—who is also a perfect stranger—rushes up and kisses you passionately before quickly disappearing. Then, another day in another city, the same gorgeous lady again appears suddenly, kisses you senseless and vanishes. Wouldn't your head be reeling? Well, those are just two of the several unique ways that Cecilia St. Martin gets to Abbott. You will relish this wildly wonderful, very touching romance from Linda who makes her truly stylish, truly nifty debut as a romance writer with us.

And last, but never, never least is the beautiful romance **JOURNEY'S END,** LOVESWEPT #146, by Joan Elliott Pickart. In this dramatic and tender love story Victoria Blair finds everything she ever dreamed of having in the arms of Sage Lawson, owner of the Lazy L ranch just outside Sunshine, New Mexico. Indeed at times sunshine does seem to pour down on these two lovely people who appear to be made in heaven for each other. Yet ominous clouds of doubt and misunderstanding threaten their budding love. Sage

(continued)

grows hostile, Blair becomes distant, withdrawn. Clearly they need a little push back into one another's arms . . . and the matchmakers and the ways they give that little push are sure to delight you.

As always, we hope that each of these four LOVE-SWEPTs will give you the greatest of pleasure.

With warm good wishes,

Carolyn Nichols

Carolyn Nichols
  Editor
LOVESWEPT
Bantam Books, Inc.
666 Fifth Avenue
New York, NY 10103

LOVESWEPT

Love Stories you'll never forget by authors you'll always remember